New York Times and USA TODAY bestselling author
Brenda Jackson

"Brenda Jackson writes romance that sizzles
and characters you fall in love with."
—*New York Times* and *USA TODAY* bestselling author
Lori Foster

"Jackson's trademark ability to weave
multiple characters and side stories together
makes shocking truths all the more exciting."
—*Publishers Weekly*

"There is no getting away from the sex appeal and
charm of Jackson's Westmoreland family."
—*RT Book Reviews* on *Feeling the Heat*

"Jackson's characters are wonderful, strong,
colorful and hot enough to burn the pages."
—*RT Book Reviews* on *Westmoreland's Way*

"The kind of sizzling, heart-tugging story
Brenda Jackson is famous for."
—*RT Book Reviews* on *Spencer's Forbidden Passion*

"This is entertainment at its best."
—*RT Book Reviews* on *Star of His Heart*

* * *

Canyon is part of The Westmorelands series:
A family bound by loyalty...and love!

Dear Reader,

I love writing about those Westmorelands because they exemplify what a strong family is all about, mainly the sharing of love and support. For that reason, when I was given the chance to present them in a trilogy, I was excited and ready to dive into the lives of Zane, Canyon and Stern Westmoreland.

It is hard to believe that Canyon is my twenty-fifth Westmoreland novel. It seems like it was only yesterday when I introduced you to Delaney and her five brothers. I knew by the time I wrote Thorn's story that I just had to tell you about their cousins that were spread out over Montana, Texas, California and Colorado.

It has been an adventure and I enjoyed sharing it with you. I've gotten your emails and snail mails letting me know how much you adore those Westmoreland men, and I appreciate hearing from you. Each Westmoreland—male or female—is unique, and the way love conquers their hearts is heartwarming, breathtaking and totally satisfying.

In this story, Canyon is in for a shocker when he discovers his former girlfriend's closely guarded secret. And then he has to learn to forgive a woman who has a problem with forgiving herself.

I hope you enjoy this story about Canyon and Keisha Ashford.

Happy Reading!

Brenda Jackson

BRENDA JACKSON

Canyon

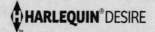
HARLEQUIN® DESIRE

To my husband, the love of my life and my best friend, Gerald Jackson, Sr.

To the members of the Brenda Jackson Support Team, this one is for you!

A merry heart doeth good like a medicine: but a broken spirit drieth the bones.
—*Proverbs* 17:22

ISBN-13: 978-0-373-73258-6

CANYON

Copyright © 2013 by Brenda Streater Jackson

Recycling programs for this product may not exist in your area.

Printed in U.S.A.

www.Harlequin.com

Other titles by this author
are available in ebook format.

BRENDA JACKSON

is a die "heart" romantic who married her childhood sweetheart and still proudly wears the "going steady" ring he gave her when she was fifteen. Because she believes in the power of love, Brenda's stories always have happy endings. In her real-life love story, Brenda and her husband of more than forty years live in Jacksonville, Florida, and have two sons.

A *New York Times* bestselling author of more than seventy-five romance titles, Brenda is a recent retiree who now divides her time between family, writing and traveling with Gerald. You may write Brenda at P.O. Box 28267, Jacksonville, Florida 32226, email her at WriterBJackson@aol.com or visit her website at www.brendajackson.net.

THE DENVER WESTMORELAND FAMILY TREE

Raphel and Gemma Westmoreland

Stern Westmoreland (Paula Bailey)

Thomas (Susan)

Adam (Clarisse)

Micah (Kalina) ③
Jason (Bella) ④
Riley (Alpha) ⑧
Canyon (Keisha) ⑩
Stern
Brisbane

Dillon (Pamela) ①

Ramsey (Chloe) ②
Zane (Channing) ⑨
Derringer (Lucia) ④
Megan (Rico) ⑦
Gemma (Callum) ③
Adrian
Aidan
Bailey

① *Westmoreland's Way*
② *Hot Westmoreland Nights*
③ *What a Westmoreland Wants*
④ *A Wife for a Westmoreland*
⑤ *The Proposal*

⑥ *Feeling the Heat*
⑦ *Texas Wild*
⑧ *One Winter's Night*
⑨ *Zane*
⑩ *Canyon*

One

Canyon Westmoreland was tempted to get out of the parked car and stretch his legs, but decided against it. The one thing he'd learned from watching cop shows was that when you were on a stakeout, you did nothing to give yourself away. You remained as inconspicuous as possible. And as far as he was concerned, he was on a stakeout, determined to find out once and for all why Keisha Ashford refused to give him the time of day.

He was very much aware that she hated his guts because she believed he had betrayed her with another woman. And he knew that assumption was the reason she'd left town three years ago, cutting all ties with him, and was also the reason why she felt that, upon returning to Denver, she had every right to act as if he didn't exist.

However, he had put up with it long enough.

They were both corporate attorneys, a profession which had brought them together initially, and a profession that still placed them together on a number of occasions. Since she'd returned to Denver ten months ago, they'd sat across from each other at the negotiating table for more than one business deal. And it bothered him when she acted as if they didn't share a past.

A number of times he had approached her about straightening things out between them, if for no other reason than so they could have closure, but she always turned him down.

Well, he'd had enough. He refused to allow another day to go by with her thinking he had betrayed her.

So here he was, parked outside the law firm where she worked. Canyon planned to follow her home and confront her. They would finally have that discussion she'd been refusing to give him.

His brothers Stern and Riley had warned him that she had the right to call the police if she felt harassed. But he hoped she wouldn't feel that way. He wasn't trying to harass her. He only wanted to talk to her.

He glanced at his watch. Since he wasn't sure what time she got off work, he'd been parked here for more than an hour now, leaving early from his job at his family's company—Blue Ridge Land Management—to make sure he didn't miss her.

He'd moved to switch channels on the radio when his cell phone rang. He pulled it out of his pocket and frowned when he saw it was his brother. He clicked the phone on.

"What do you want, Stern?"

"Just calling to see if you've been arrested yet."

Canyon rolled his eyes. "I won't be getting arrested."

"Don't be too sure of that. No woman likes being stalked."

Canyon's hand tightened on the steering wheel. "I'm not stalking her."

Stern chuckled. "So what do you call your plan of waiting in front of her office with the intention of following her home?"

Canyon adjusted his tall frame in the seat to find a more comfortable position. "I wouldn't have to follow her if she'd told me where she lives."

"There's a chance the reason she didn't tell you is because she doesn't want you to know," Stern said. "Her house is her territory, and you're forcing yourself into her space. She might not like that."

Canyon was about to tell his brother that at this point he couldn't care less about what she liked when he saw Keisha and another woman walk out of the building together. They were conversing and smiling, headed to their cars. Both were nice-looking women, but his gaze was focused solely on Keisha. He thought the same thing now that he'd thought the first time he'd met her. She was an incredibly beautiful woman.

She still had creamy brown skin that highlighted dark brown eyes, a perky nose and high cheekbones. And she still wore her silky black hair straight and parted in the center. It brushed against her shoulders. Just looking at her full lips made him remember how they tasted, which in turn made him hungry for them. He wished he didn't recall the many times he'd spent devouring her mouth.

But there was something different about her shapely body in that navy A-line skirt and pretty blue blouse. Was it his imagination, or did her hips really appear curvier and her breasts slightly larger than what he remembered?

Regardless of whether his memory was playing tricks on him or not, Keisha Ashford looked good.

He shifted in his seat again, thinking some things didn't change, even his desire for a woman who couldn't stand him.

But he had no problem remembering a time when she *could* stand him. Those had been the best times of his life. He'd never thought he would be ready to settle down with a woman before his thirty-fifth birthday, but he had fallen for Keisha quickly and had been ready to pop the question—before a lie had torn them apart.

He released a deep sigh as his gaze continued to soak her in, every single detail, especially those legs, which could wrap so firmly around a man's waist—

"Canyon, are you still there?"

He blinked upon remembering he still had Stern on the phone. "Yes, I'm here. But I have to go. Keisha just walked out and I need to follow her."

"Be careful, bro. It's been a long time since a Westmoreland was put in jail. I'm sure you remember those days."

He drew in a deep breath. How could he forget? There was only one Westmoreland with a jail record. As a teen, his baby brother Brisbane—known around Denver as *Badass Bane*—had gotten into enough trouble for all of them. Now Bane was serving his country as a kicking-the-enemy-ass navy SEAL.

"It won't get that far, Stern. I'm no threat to Keisha. I just want to talk to her."

"You weren't a threat to her before, but that didn't stop her from almost slapping a restraining order on you. Look, Canyon, it's your business but—"

"I know, I know, Stern. You don't want me to do anything to bring shame on the family."

Keisha and the woman had parted ways, and Keisha was now walking alone toward her car. She still had that walk that he thought was as sexy as hell. Although she moved like a model, she had the look of a cool professional in her four-inch pumps with her briefcase in hand.

"Canyon!"

He jumped. "Look, Stern. I'll call you later."

Without giving his brother a chance to say anything else, Canyon clicked off the phone. He watched as Keisha sized up her surroundings before opening her car and getting inside. Although she had glanced in his direction she hadn't seen him. He was parked behind a couple of cars.

He gave her time to start her car and pull out of her parking spot. Then, just as he was about to pull out of his own parking spot, a car darted out in front of him.

"What the hell," Canyon muttered, hitting his brakes. "What damn fire is he rushing off to?"

Not wanting to lose Keisha, he pulled in behind the black sedan, keeping her vehicle within his vision. After tailing her for a few blocks, he became uneasy. It seemed the car in front of him—the black sedan—was tailing her, as well.

As an attorney, Canyon was aware there were times when clients of the opposing council didn't like a court's decision and wanted to make that dislike known. That could be what was happening here. He didn't want to think of other possibilities, like a carjacking. They'd had a number of those lately around the city.

Canyon's protective instincts kicked in when Keisha turned a corner to head away from town and the driver of the black sedan did, too. He couldn't tell if the person driving the car in front of him was male or female because the windows were tinted. But he *could* make out the license plate number.

He pushed the phone button on his steering wheel. "Yes, Mr. Westmoreland, may I help you?"

"Yes, Samuel. Please connect me with Pete Higgins."

Pete was best friends with his cousin Derringer and was a deputy with Denver's police department.

"Please hold on for the connection."

It didn't take long for Pete to come on the line. "Deputy Higgins."

"Pete. This is Canyon. I need you to check out a license plate number."

"Why?"

Although Canyon knew Pete had every right to ask that question, he couldn't keep his irritation from escalating. "A woman is being followed."

"And you know this how?"

Canyon bit his lip to keep from cursing. His patience was stretched to the limit. "I know because I'm following her, as well."

"Oh. And why arc *you* following her?"

Canyon had always admired Pete's easy, laid-back manner. Until now. "Now look, Pete."

"No, you look, Canyon. No one should be following a woman, not you or anybody else. That's harassment and I can bring you both in for stalking. What's the license plate number?"

A mad-as-hell Canyon rattled off the number while wondering why Keisha hadn't noticed she was being followed by not one, but two vehicles.

"Um, this is interesting," Pete said.

"What?" Canyon asked, annoyed.

"That license plate was stolen."

"Stolen?"

The driver in the sedan was smart enough not to follow behind Keisha too closely. But evidently he wasn't smart enough to pick up on the fact that he or she was being followed by Canyon. Maybe the driver was so busy keeping up with Keisha that he hadn't noticed what was going on behind him.

"Yes. According to our system, that license plate was reported stolen earlier today. Where are you?"

"Right now I'm going through the intersection of Fire-stone Road and Tinsel, and heading toward Purcell Park Road."

"You're way on the other side of town," Pete noted.

"Yeah." Canyon wondered if Keisha had deliberately chosen to live on the opposite side of Denver from where the Westmorelands lived.

"Is she driving a nice car?" Pete asked.

"Yes, looks like a pretty new Bimmer. Why?"

"I'm thinking that you might be looking at a possible carjacking. I'm on my way. Don't do anything stupid until I get there."

Canyon rolled his eyes. Did that mean he could do something stupid *after* Pete got there?

The thought of someone stalking Keisha angered him, and he quickly pushed to the back of his mind the thought that he was doing basically the same thing. The big difference was that Canyon didn't intend to hurt one single hair on Keisha's head. He couldn't say the same for the bozo in front of him.

The last thing the other driver needed to know was where she lived. If she was heading home, he didn't have time to wait for Pete. Pete's office was on the other side of town. There was no telling how long it would take him to get here. At that moment, Canyon made a decision.

He would handle the situation himself.

Keisha swayed her body to the music blaring out of her car radio. She loved satellite stations with continuous commercial-free music, and she especially liked this channel, which played her favorite hits nonstop. And today she needed to hear them.

It had been one of those kinds of days.

It had started at ten, in court. She'd barely had time to

grab lunch before rushing back to the courthouse for another case at one. Around three, she had returned to her
office only to be pulled into a meeting she'd forgotten
about. She was glad to have left work to start what would
be a busy weekend.

Even knowing everything she had to do over the next
two days did not dampen her mood. She'd won three cases
this week, and she knew her bosses, Leonard Spivey and
Adam Whitlock, were pleased.

Three years ago, Leonard hadn't liked it when she'd
given him only a week's notice before leaving Denver and
moving back home to Texas. But because she'd been one
of the firm's best attorneys, he'd been kind enough to give
her a very good recommendation—and to welcome her
back to the firm when she'd needed to return.

Sometimes things happened for a reason. When she'd
moved to Texas, it hadn't taken her long to land another job
at a law firm in Austin. And had she not returned home,
she probably would not have found out about her mother's
breast cancer scare.

Luckily, Keisha had been there for her mother during
that difficult time. The two of them had always been close.
Lynn Ashford was a strong and independent single parent. After the man who'd fathered Keisha denied she was
his, Lynn had moved away from her hometown of Austin and settled with her daughter in Baton Rouge. Then,
when Keisha's grandfather had died when she was fifteen,
she and her mother had returned to Austin to be there for
Keisha's grandmother.

There had been many hard times while growing up.
To compensate, her mother had worked two jobs, leaving
Keisha in the care of her grandmother. But seeing how
hard her mother had worked without the help of a man

had shown Keisha that if push came to shove, she could do the same.

Her heart ached when she thought about the man who had proved that fact to her.

Canyon Westmoreland.

She'd fallen in love with him the first day she'd laid eyes on him, but that love ended when she discovered he'd been unfaithful to her. She could tolerate a lot of things, but the one thing she wouldn't tolerate was infidelity. Trust was paramount and a loss of it meant an end to everything... even a relationship that had held so much promise. Or she'd thought it'd had promise. Obviously she had been wrong.

Now, after three years, she was back in Denver. The scandal that had hit the law firm where she'd worked in Austin, and the firm's eventual shutdown by the Texas Bar and the justice department, had made leaving a necessity. She'd known she would miss her mom, and that she was taking a chance with her decision to return to Denver, but Spivey and Whitlock was the one law office where she wouldn't have to start at the bottom. She needed the money because she had more than herself to think about these days. However, to assure that she didn't run into Canyon, other than for business, she'd deliberately moved clear on the other side of town from Westmoreland Country.

She knew the story of how Canyon's parents, aunt and uncle had died in a plane crash, leaving fifteen orphans. Staying together hadn't been easy, especially since several of the siblings and cousins had been under the age of sixteen. But together, the Westmoreland family had weathered hard times and was now enjoying the good times thanks to the success of the family's land management firm, Blue Ridge.

Canyon's parents had had seven sons: Dillon, Micah,

Jason, Riley, Canyon, Stern and Brisbane. His aunt and uncle had had eight children: five boys—Ramsey, Zane, Derringer and the twins Aiden and Adrian; and three girls—Megan, Gemma and Bailey. From what Keisha knew, the majority of the Westmorelands were now college educated and successful in their own right, either working for the family firm or in their chosen profession. She'd met most of them when she had attended the annual Westmoreland Ball while she was dating Canyon. The ball was a huge event in the city and benefited a number of charities.

Her thoughts shifted back to one Westmoreland in particular. Canyon.

The *Grand Canyon,* as she would sometimes call him during more intimate moments.

The memories of those times hurt the most. She had loved him and had believed he loved her. She had opened her heart, and her home, to him. He had moved in with her after they'd dated for six months. She'd assumed their relationship was moving in the right direction. He had proved her wrong.

The blaring of a horn prompted her to glance in her rearview mirror. *What in the world?* she asked herself, frowning.

The drivers of the two cars behind her were engaging in some kind of road rage. It appeared that the driver of a burgundy car was trying to run the driver of a black sedan off the road.

Deciding the last thing she needed was to get involved in what was going on with those two drivers, she increased her speed and drove on ahead, leaving behind what she perceived as two hotheads vying to be king of the road.

Keisha checked the clock on the dashboard. She was eager to reach her destination and the person waiting for her there.

* * *

Canyon watched the black sedan speed off. Although he'd gotten pretty close to the car, the tinted windows had prevented him from determining if the driver had been a man or a woman, but he was leaning more toward a man.

He returned his attention to the road in time to see Keisha turn the corner a couple of blocks ahead. He continued to keep his distance, not wanting her to know she was being followed. It had been a long time since he'd been in this section of Denver, but because of the nature of his business, he knew about all the new development in the area. Several housing communities had been constructed, along with a number of shopping places and restaurants.

He watched Keisha put on her car's right blinker to turn into what he at first thought was a doctor's complex. Upon getting a better view of the huge sign out front, he saw it was Mary's Little Lamb Day Care. He frowned. Why would she be stopping at a day care? Maybe she was doing one of her coworkers a favor by picking up their child, or she could have volunteered to babysit tonight for someone.

He slid into a parking spot and watched as she got out of her car and went inside, smiling. That probably meant she was ready for the weekend to begin. Hopefully, her good mood would continue when she saw that he'd followed her home. His focus stayed on her, concentrating on the sway of her hips with every step she took, until she was no longer in sight.

He was about to change stations on his radio when his cell phone rang. He hoped it wasn't Stern again. He pulled it out of his pocket and saw it was his cousin Bailey, the youngest of the Westmoreland siblings and cousins living in Denver. Growing up, Bailey had been nearly as bad as Bane when it came to getting into trouble.

He clicked the phone on. "What's up, Bay?"

"Zane's back. He got in today."

Canyon nodded. His cousin Zane had left town a good three weeks ago on what Canyon had assumed was a business trip, only to discover later that his cousin was running behind a woman he'd once had an affair with by the name of Channing Hastings. Rumor had it that Zane was returning home with a wedding band on his finger.

"He's married?"

"Not yet. He and Channing are talking about a Christmas wedding."

A Christmas wedding? It was hard to believe Zane, a die-hard bachelor, was thinking about settling down.

"Didn't think I'd live to see the day."

"Well, I'm glad he came to his senses." Bailey paused and then said, "Don't forget this is chow-down night."

Every other Friday night, the Westmorelands got together at his brother Dillon's place. The women would do the cooking and the men would arrive hungry. Afterward, the men took part in a poker game and the women did whatever they pleased.

"I might be a little late," he said, since he wasn't sure how his confrontation with Keisha would go. If she was babysitting somebody's kid, he would follow her home just to see where she lived and then return at another time and try to talk to her. At some point, he needed to let her know about the person who'd been following her. It might be something she needed to check into, especially if it was related to a case she was working on.

"Why?"

He frowned at Bailey's question. "Why what?"

"Why will you be late? Dillon mentioned you left work early today."

For some reason Bailey assumed being the youngest automatically made her privy to everyone's business. Instead of answering her, he tapped on the phone several times and then said, "Sounds like we have a bad connection, Bay. I'll talk to you later."

He clicked the phone off in time to see Keisha walk back out of the building. Studying her face he saw she was still smiling, which was a good sign. She was also chatting with the little boy whose hand she was holding—a boy who was probably around two years old.

Canyon studied the little boy's features. "WTF," he muttered under his breath. The kid could be a double for Denver, Dillon's three-year-old son. In fact, if Canyon didn't know for certain that Denver was at home with Dillon's wife, Pam, he would think it was Denver's hand that Keisha was holding. An uneasy feeling stirred his insides as he continued to study the little boy whose smile was just as big as Keisha's.

Canyon took in a gasping breath. There was only one reason the little boy looked so much like a Westmoreland. Canyon gripped the steering wheel, certain steam was coming out of his ears and nose.

He didn't remember easing his seat back, unbuckling his seat belt or opening the car door. Neither did he remember walking toward Keisha. However, he would always remember the look on her face when she stopped walking and glanced in his direction. What he saw in her features was surprise, guilt and remorse.

As he got closer he watched defensiveness followed by fierce protectiveness replace those other emotions. She stopped walking and pulled her son—the child he was certain was *their* son—closer to her side. "What are you doing here, Canyon?"

He came to a stop in front of her. His body was radiating anger from the inside out. His gaze left her face and looked down at the little boy who was clutching the hem of

Keisha's skirt and staring up at him with distrustful eyes
that were almost identical to his mother's.

Canyon shifted his gaze back up to meet Keisha's eyes.
In a voice shaking with fury, he asked, "Would you like
to tell me why I didn't know I had a son?"

Two

Keisha drew in a deep breath while thinking about what she would say, and from Canyon's tone of voice she knew it better be good. She'd often wondered how he would react when he found out he had a son. Would he deny her child was his like her own father had done with her?

Instead of answering his question, she countered with one of her own. "Would it have mattered had you known?"

She saw surprise flash in his eyes just seconds before his lips formed a tight line. "Of course it would have mattered," he said with affront. "Now tell me why I wasn't told."

Keisha could tell by the way her son held tight to her skirt that he sensed something was wrong, and she knew how anxious he got around strangers. Although she wished otherwise, the time had come for her and Canyon to talk. But not now and not here.

"I need to get Beau home and—"

"Beau?"

She lifted her chin. "Yes. My son's name is Beau Ashford."

The anger that flashed across his face was quick. And although he muttered the words, "Not for long," under his breath, she heard them.

She slowly pulled in a deep breath and then carefully exhaled it. "Like I said, Canyon. I need to get Beau home to prepare dinner and then—"

"Fine," he cut in before she finished. "Whatever you have planned for tonight, I'm included."

Like hell he was. "Now look here, Canyon. I—"

She stopped talking when she saw Pauline Sampson, owner of the day care, approaching them. Pauline had been one of Keisha's first clients when she'd begun practicing law five years ago. She was also a friend of Mr. Spivey's wife, Joan. Pauline was smiling but Keisha saw deep concern in every curve of the woman's lips. There was also a degree of curiosity in her eyes.

"Keisha, I happened to glance out my window and saw you were still here. I just wanted to make sure everything was okay," Pauline said smoothly.

If everything wasn't okay, Keisha had no intention of letting Pauline know. "Yes, everything is fine, Pauline." She hadn't planned on making introductions, and she was aware that Canyon knew it. She really wasn't surprised when he took it upon himself to make the introductions himself.

Extending his hand out to Pauline, he said, "How are you, Pauline? I'm Canyon Westmoreland, Beau's father."

Keisha watched Pauline's brow lift in surprise. "Westmoreland?"

Canyon flashed Pauline what Keisha knew to be his

dashing smile, one known to win over jurors in the courtroom. "Yes, Westmoreland."

She saw interest shine in Pauline's eyes. "Are you related to Dillon Westmoreland?"

Canyon kept his smile in place. "Yes, Dillon is my oldest brother."

Pauline's smile widened. "Small world. I can definitely see the resemblance. Dillon and I went to high school together and serve on the boards of directors of several businesses in town."

"Yes, it is a small world," Canyon agreed, glancing at his watch. "If you don't mind excusing us, Pauline, Keisha and I need to get Beau home for dinner."

"Oh, not at all," Pauline said, beaming. "I understand." She then glanced up at Keisha. "Have a good weekend."

Keisha doubted that would happen now. "You, too, Pauline."

She knew not to waste time talking Canyon out of following her home. He wanted her to answer his question—not tomorrow or next week, but tonight.

When Pauline turned to go back inside, Keisha moved toward her car and gasped in surprise when Canyon reached down and picked up Beau. Keisha opened her mouth to warn him that Beau didn't take well to strangers. She closed it when instead of screaming at the top of his lungs, Beau wrapped his arms around Canyon's neck.

Canyon adjusted their son in his arms. "I'll carry him to the car for you."

She frowned. "He can walk."

"I know he can, but I want to carry him. Humor me."

Keisha didn't want to humor him. She didn't want to have anything to do with him. Father or no father, if Canyon thought he could bombard his way into her or Beau's lives, he had another think coming. He'd made his choice three years ago.

She tried pushing her mother's warning to the back of her mind. When Keisha had discovered her pregnancy and shared the news with her mother, Lynn had warned her not to assume Canyon would be like Kenneth Drew. Lynn believed every man had a right to know he'd fathered a child, which is why she had told Kenneth. Only after his decision not to accept Keisha as his child had Lynn ceased including Kenneth in her daughter's life.

Lynn felt Keisha hadn't given Canyon a chance to either accept or reject his child, and he should be given that choice. Keisha hadn't felt that way. Knowing her father had rejected her had tormented her all through childhood and right into her adult life. It had been her decision to never let her son experience the grief of rejection.

When they reached her car, she opened the door to the backseat and moved aside to watch Canyon place Beau in his car seat. Then another surprise happened. Beau actually protested and tried reaching for Canyon to get back into his arms.

"It seems he likes you," Keisha muttered, truly not happy with it at all.

Canyon glanced over his shoulder at her. "It's a Westmoreland thing."

Keisha didn't say anything. If that was his way of letting her know his son should have been born with his name, he'd done so effectively.

"From now on, partner, I'll never be too far away," she heard him say to Beau and wondered if he realized he needed her permission for that to happen. When it came to her son, he would only have the rights she gave him.

As if Beau understood, he then spoke to Canyon for

the first time. Pointing his finger at himself, he said, "Me Beau." He then pointed at Canyon. "You?"

Canyon chuckled and Keisha knew he had deliberately said the next words loud enough for her to hear. "Dad."

Beau repeated the word *dad* as if he needed to say it. "Dad."

Canyon chuckled. "Yes, Dad." He then closed the car door and turned to Keisha.

Ignoring the fierce frown on his face, she said, "You seem to be good with kids."

He shrugged. "Dillon has a son named Denver who's a little older than Beau, and I'm around him a lot. They favor."

She lifted a brow. "Who?"

"Beau and Denver. Although Denver is a little taller, if you put them in a room together it might be hard to tell them apart."

It was Keisha's time to shrug. She would know her son anywhere. Besides, she couldn't imagine the two kids looking that much alike. "Since you insist that we need to talk today, you can follow me home. But I don't intend to break my routine with Beau because of you."

"I don't expect you to."

She moved to walk around to the driver's side of the car when he reached out and touched her. Immediately, heat raced up her spine and she was forced to remember the raw masculine energy Canyon possessed. She'd have thought that after three years she would be immune to him, but it seemed nothing had changed in the sexual-chemistry department.

"Keisha?"

With her pulse throbbing, she fought to regain her composure. She lifted her chin. "What?"

He met her gaze and held it. "Is there any reason someone would be following you?"

"What are you talking about?" Keisha asked, frowning.

Canyon shoved his hands into his pockets. "I started
following you from your job, but I wasn't the only one. A
black sedan pulled out in front of me and whoever was behind the wheel followed you until a mile or so back. That's
when I tried getting the driver's attention by driving close
along the side of the car and forcing him or her to pull over.
I don't know if the driver was a man or a woman since
the windows were tinted. Instead of pulling over, the car
made a quick right turn at the next corner and kept going."

Keisha remembered glancing in her rearview mirror and
witnessing what she'd assumed were two drivers engaging
in road rage. "You're driving a burgundy car?"

"Yes."

"I heard a horn blast and saw you trying to run that
black car off the road. I figured it was nothing more than
two drivers acting like fools."

"It wasn't. It was about me trying to find out why someone was following you. I even called the police to report it."

"The police?"

"Yes. Just so happens that Pete Higgins is a deputy and
a friend of Derringer's. At the time, I only had a hunch
you were being followed, so Pete checked it out as a favor.
Then he got suspicious when he discovered the license
plate had been reported as stolen. He's since phoned back
to say they're still looking for the car."

Although Keisha had only met Derringer Westmoreland
once, during the Westmoreland Ball, she'd heard about
him. Before marrying and settling down, he'd had a reputation of being quite the ladies' man. In fact, a number of
male Westmorelands had claimed that reputation.

"Well, I have no idea why anyone would be following me. Why were you following me?"

"Because on a number of occasions over the past ten months, I've approached you, wanting to talk and you refused to give me the time of day. Now I know why."

Not wanting to get into it with Canyon about Beau now, because she was certain Pauline probably had her face glued to her office window, Keisha said, "We'll talk later."

"I'll be right behind you."

Canyon waited until Keisha had gotten into her car before crossing the parking lot to get into his. It was only when he had closed the door and snapped his seat belt that the impact of the past twenty minutes hit him hard.

He had a son. A son he hadn't known about until today.

With her heart pounding furiously in her chest, Keisha pulled out of the day care's parking lot. She thought about Canyon's assertion that a car had been following her. That didn't make sense. None of the cases she was working on were serious enough to warrant anyone wanting to harass her.

This was a new car she was driving, a very popular model. Perhaps the person had had carjacking in mind? Shivers raced through her at the thought.

When she came to a traffic light she glanced into the backseat to make sure Beau was okay. She couldn't get over how easily he had accepted Canyon.

And just how easily Canyon had accepted him.

Canyon hadn't demanded a DNA test for verification, instead he'd claimed that Beau favored Dillon's son. Had that been the reason why his acceptance had come without any hassles? Well, there hadn't been any hassles so far. They still had to talk, and someone who'd been as close to Canyon as she had been in the past knew that while he had a cool demeanor on the outside, he was simmering on the inside.

Keisha drew in a deep breath and exited onto the road that would take her home. Glancing in the rearview mirror her gaze met Canyon's as he seemed to look right at her. Gee whiz, did he have to look at her like that? With an intensity that had her dragging in more than one shaky breath and a rush of heat flooding her stomach, making it quiver. She gripped the steering wheel and refocused on her driving.

Canyon had always been able to get to her. At that moment, she couldn't help but remember the day nearly four years ago when they'd met...

"Excuse me. Is this seat taken?"

Keisha looked up from the papers she'd been reading. A shot of hard lust reverberated through her veins. Lordy. Standing in front of her had to be, without a doubt, a man who could get a "yes" out of a woman without even asking the first question.

He was tall, more than six feet, and she had to strain her neck to look up at him. He had smooth mahogany skin, dark eyes, a firm jaw and a too-delicious-looking pair of lips. Once she got past his facial features then she had to deal with his broad shoulders and a too-fine body in an immaculate business suit.

"So, is it?" he asked in a deep, sexy voice.

She self-consciously licked her lips. "Is what?"

"This seat taken? It seems to be the only one empty."

She glanced around the courthouse's lunchroom. He was telling the truth. "No, it's not taken."

"Mind if I join you?"

She had to bite her lips to keep from saying he could

do anything he cared to do with her. Instead, she said, "No, I don't mind."

She watched as he pulled out a chair and settled his tall frame in the seat. She had to be in court in less than an hour. At any other time she would have been annoyed at being disturbed, but not this time. This man was worth the interruption.

Extending his hand out to her, he said, "I'm Canyon Westmoreland. And you are?"

"Keisha. Keisha Ashford." She accepted his hand and wished she hadn't. Her belly vibrated the moment they touched. And then, suddenly, it seemed the room quieted and they were the only two people in it. The only thing she heard was the sound of their breathing. The way he stared into her eyes made her breath catch. She felt the rush through her veins.

The sound of silverware hitting the floor made her blink, and she realized Canyon still had her hand. She tugged and he released it.

"So, Keisha Ashford, are you an attorney or a paralegal?"

She lifted a brow. "Does it matter?"

He shrugged broad shoulders. "Not with me. I'm sharing a table with a beautiful woman and I'm not complaining about anything."

She chuckled, appreciating his compliment. "You sound easy."

"Um, maybe."

A smile spread across her lips. She liked him. She had checked out his ring finger. It was bare, with no indication that a ring had once been there. "I'm an attorney."

"So am I," he said smoothly.

"I can tell. You look the part," she said.

He leaned over the table and she drew in his intoxicat-

ing male scent. "Let's meet later so you can tell me what you mean by that."

Oh, she thought. He was good. As smooth as silk. Any other time, and with anyone else, she would have brushed off what was definitely a flirtatious come-on. But not today. And, for some reason, not with Canyon West-moreland.

Instead of agreeing to his suggestion, she said, "Canyon is an unusual name."

"Not according to my parents," he said, smiling. "I was conceived one night in the Grand Canyon, so they felt my name fit. I understand it was one hell of a night."

She tilted her head. "Your parents told you that?"

"No, but I heard them share a private joke about it every once in a while. It brought them fond memories for years."

"And what do they think now?"

She saw a flash of pain flare in his eyes. "I don't know. My parents were killed in a plane crash a little over fifteen years ago."

"Oh, I'm sorry," she said.

"Thanks. Now what about meeting me later for drinks? There's a place not far from here. Woody's." He glanced at his watch. "Around five. Hopefully, if we win our individual cases, we will have reason to celebrate."

She smiled. "That would be nice. I'll be there."

He tipped his head and the smile that spread across his lips was priceless...and sexy as hell. "Good. I'll look forward to later, Keisha Ashford."

She swallowed as his gaze raked over her in a way that had her skin scorching. At that moment she was drenched in full awareness of him and could only respond by saying truthfully, "So will I...."

"Mommy."

Keisha's thoughts returned to the present at the sound of her son's voice. He had been busy playing with one of his toys while sitting in his car seat. Beau was just as high-spirited as any other two-year-old and typically never stopped talking except when shoving food into his mouth. But today things were different. She couldn't help wondering if Canyon's presence had something to do with it.

"Yes, Beau?"

"Dad gone?"

Was that disappointment she heard in his voice? Moving here from Texas had been hard for him. Her mother had become a regular fixture in his life and the first months away from his grandmother hadn't been easy. Beau had made her fully aware what tantrums were about.

"He's in the car behind us."

She looked in the mirror and saw Beau trying to twist his body around in his car seat. "Why?"

She lifted a brow. "Why?"

"He not here. Our car?"

Keisha felt a headache coming on and knew after Canyon's visit she would have to have a talk with her son. "Because he has his own car."

"Go home with us?"

"Yes." Too late she realized how that sounded and quickly moved to clear it up. "He has his own home. Not ours."

"Not our house?"

"No, not our house."

He didn't say anything, but went back to playing with his toy. When they got home she would feed him dinner, give him a bath and then let him have a little playtime before putting him in bed. When it came to bedtime, she was lucky. Beau didn't have the issues some other kids did with

fighting sleep. He eagerly went to bed each night as if it
was his God-given right to get eight hours or more of sleep.

She glanced back into her rearview mirror at the car
still following closely behind her. Her gaze connected with
Canyon's once again.

She no longer loved him, she was sure of it. Her love
hadn't dissipated immediately but in slow degrees. And
just to think—she had planned to tell him about her pregnancy when she had returned home early and found him
with Bonita.

She broke eye contact to face the road ahead, which is
what she'd been doing since that night. And she didn't intend to look back again.

Moments later she was pulling into the driveway of the
home she considered hers. The community was a new one,
and most of the families were progressive couples or sin-
gles with small children. She'd already joined the homeowners association and knew several of her neighbors. It
was a friendly neighborhood and she enjoyed living here.

She brought the car to a stop and then got out. She had
moved around to the side of the car by the time Canyon
got out of his. She glanced over at him and said, "I really
wish you'd wait and talk to me at another time."

"We don't always get what we want, Keisha."

Feeling frustrated and annoyed, she narrowed her eyes
at him and opened the door to get Beau out of his seat.

"I'll do that," Canyon said.

She stepped aside to let him, not wanting to make a
scene in front of Beau. However, the main thing she intended to do when they talked was to make it absolutely
clear that while he might be Beau's father, she would not
allow him to bulldoze his way into their lives.

Pulling her keys from her purse, she moved up the walk-
way to her front door. Canyon followed with Beau in his

arms. She was tempted to remind Canyon once again that Beau could walk, but decided to keep quiet for now.

The moment she opened the door, Keisha knew something was wrong. For starters, the chime from her security alarm didn't sound. And when she took a step inside and glanced around, she gasped in horror.

Someone had broken into her home.

Three

Canyon quickly went into action and handed Beau to Keisha. "Take Beau and get back in the car."

Already he was on the phone calling Pete. "This is Canyon. The woman who was being followed earlier today had her home broken into."

"What's the address? I'm still in the area. Don't mess with anything."

Canyon turned around, not surprised that Keisha hadn't gone back to the car like he'd told her to do. "What's the address?" He could tell from her dazed look that she was still in shock at what she'd found when she'd opened her door.

"Keisha?"

She looked at him. "Yes?"

"What's this address?"

She rattled a number off to him which he gave to Pete.

"Home messy, Mommy."

Their son's words made Keisha suck in a deep breath and Canyon saw how Beau's innocent words had crushed her. This was the home she had made for her and their son and someone had invaded her sanctuary. They had violated it.

"Come on, let's step outside, Keisha. The police are on the way," he said softly. When she opened her mouth to protest, he added, "We can't touch anything until they get here."

Keisha closed her mouth and drew in a deep breath, feeling the pain in her chest when she did so. Canyon, she knew, was intentionally blocking her view but she'd already seen her living room and could just imagine how the rest of her house looked. Had the intruder gone into her bedroom? Beau's room? What had been stolen?

"Keisha?"

"Yes?" The single word had been hard to get past her lungs.

"Come on, let's sit in the car."

She hesitated but knew what he was suggesting was reasonable. There was nothing they could do until the police arrived and Beau could tell she was troubled. She didn't want to upset him.

"Play, Mommy," Beau said when they reached her car. She placed him back in his car seat and gave him his favorite toy. When she went around to get into her seat, she noticed Canyon talking on his cell phone. Was he talking to the police again?

"Yes, Keisha's okay, Dil," Canyon told his oldest brother. He'd given Dillon a quick rundown on what had transpired over the past hour, including the fact that he had a son.

"Everyone is here for dinner, so how do you want me

to handle things?" Dillon asked. "I'm sure you'll want to be the one to tell them about Beau."

Canyon drew in a deep breath. "Yes, I want to be the one. Pete is on the way. When we finish here, Keisha and Beau are coming with me until we figure out who did this and why. I'm leaving my car here so I'll need someone to pick it up and drive it to my place later."

"I can do that. But will Keisha agree to go anywhere with you, Canyon?"

Canyon rubbed a frustrated hand down his face. He was more than certain she wouldn't. At least not at first. Keisha had an independent streak that she'd inherited from the single mother who had raised her. He'd always admired her ability to stand her ground and not depend on anyone for anything. But in this case things were different. She didn't have just herself to think about. She had their son.

Their son.

The thought sent an unexplainable thrill through his veins. "No, Dil, she's not going to go along with it, at least not easily. But I'm convinced what happened to her house and that car following her today are connected. My only ace is that she has Beau to think about. If it was just her she would dig in her heels."

At that moment three police cruisers pulled up and the one leading the pack was driven by Pete. "Pete's here now, Dil. I'll call you back later."

Keisha stared at the policeman in confusion. "What do you mean I was targeted personally?"

Pete leaned against the kitchen counter as he stood beside Canyon. "You've verified that nothing of value was taken, not even that container filled with gold coins sitting in plain view on the dresser in your bedroom. My only conclusion is that the person who did this didn't take anything because this is about you personally. It seems to be more or less a scare tactic."

None of this made sense. She had been grateful that her next-door neighbors, a couple with a set of twins a few months older than Beau, had come over and offered to take him to their place, feed him dinner and keep him entertained while she handled the break-in.

With Canyon and Pete by her side, she had gone from room to room taking in the devastation. Her sofa and chairs had been turned over, pillow cushions thrown about along with her magazines. In her kitchen, the person had opened a canister and floured her counters to the point where it looked like snow in August. Not one bedroom had been left untouched…not even Beau's room. Some of his favorite toys had been broken. And in her bedroom, in addition to her clothes, which had been pulled out of the drawers and strewn about, the intruder had left water running in the bathtub to flood the floors.

What Pete said was right. Nothing of value had been taken. Not the coin collection her mother had started for Beau, not the set of expensive purses in her closet or any of her big screen televisions. The only thing the person had done was trash every part of her home as if he'd been trying to make a statement. However, she was clueless as to what statement that could be.

"Think hard, Ms. Ashford. Are there any cases you're working on that someone would want to scare you away from?" Pete asked.

For the life of her she couldn't think of one case, past or present, where anyone could want to extract some kind of revenge. She had won all her cases lately, except for one, and none of the cases were such that either party would encounter any financial hardship.

"I honestly can't think of any case like that, Deputy Higgins."

Pete nodded and shoved his notepad into his pocket. "If you think of anything later, let me know. I'm turning this over to a detective who will contact you. There is also the issue of the car that was following you earlier today, the one Canyon reported."

She'd almost forgotten about that.

"You think the two are related?" Canyon asked before she could.

"Right now, Canyon, I'm not discounting anything. By the time I reached the area where the car was supposed to be, you had taken matters into your own hands and run the guy off. I should have known it was too much to expect a Westmoreland to do what he was told."

"Whatever," Canyon said, shoving his hands into his pockets and then releasing a deep breath. "So what's next?"

"We're still looking for the vehicle. I'm going to pull the videos from the red-light cameras and traffic-surveillance cameras in the area. I hope they'll reveal something. Although we already know the license plate was stolen and the car was a black Ford sedan, if we have a picture of the vehicle itself we can determine if there are any dents or scratches that might make the car stand out. If there are, then it will make locating the vehicle easier. I want to find the person who did this."

"So do I."

Keisha and Pete looked at Canyon. It wasn't what he'd said, but how he'd said it, in a low, threatening tone. In a way, she wasn't surprised by his reaction. She'd felt the intense anger radiating from Canyon as he'd gone from room to room with her. She'd felt the hostility even more when he'd seen the senseless destruction in her and Beau's bedrooms.

Instead of either of them addressing what Canyon had said, Pete looked over at her. "I wouldn't advise you to stay here tonight. Whoever did this was able to bypass your security system."

"She won't be staying here," Canyon said before she could respond. "She's coming with me and will be staying at my place for a while."

"That's a good idea," Pete said as if that settled it.

It didn't. "Whoa. Wait a minute. I won't stay here, but I'm checking into a hotel," Keisha said.

Canyon looked at her. "No, you're not."

She placed her hands on her hips, stiffened her spine and narrowed her eyes at him. "Yes, I am."

"No, you're not."

Pete cleared his throat. "I'll let you two hash out those details without me. But if you remember anything at all, Ms. Ashford, call the precinct. Detective Ervin Render will be handling your case." Pete quickly left, as if he didn't want to get in the line of fire.

Even before Pete had cleared the doorway that separated the kitchen from the dining room, Keisha turned back to Canyon. "Now, wait just a damn minute, Canyon Westmoreland. Why should I stay with you when I can stay at a hotel? Besides, what I do or where I go is none of your business, so back off."

Hearing her sharp tone, any sane man would not have hesitated to do what she'd suggested. However, instead of backing off, Canyon took a step forward. The fierce expression on his face and the laser-sharp look in his eyes had her dropping her hands to her sides.

"Probably, if it was just you, I might back off, Keisha, since your decision about me three years ago proved just how little trust you have in me. You had the gall to believe

I would admit to loving you and then sleep with another woman…in *your* bed."

She tightened her hands into fists at her sides. "I know what I saw, Canyon."

His eyes flared with anger. "And just what did you see? Did you see me screwing Bonita? Wrapped in her arms or she in mine? No. What you saw was me, naked except for the towel wrapped around my waist, stepping out of the bathroom from my shower to find Bonita lying in your bed."

Keisha's own anger escalated. "She was naked!"

"I saw that fact at the same time you did. I told you what happened. Bonita came by your place looking for you minutes after I got in from the gym. She was upset about some argument she'd had with her fiancé, Grant Palmer, and I offered her a drink to calm her down. She asked me to share it with her and I saw no reason not to. Afterward, she thanked me, said she needed to pull herself together and asked if she could stay for a few minutes because she was too upset to drive home. I told her yes, but that I needed to take a shower. I expected her to be gone when I got out of the bathroom, because she'd said she would be."

He paused a moment and then added, "I had no idea she had stripped off her clothes and gotten into your bed until I walked out and saw you standing in the middle of the bedroom with an accusing look in your eyes. I told you the truth. But you didn't believe me. You preferred believing the lie your friend Bonita told you instead."

"Why would she lie about it? She was engaged to marry Grant."

"Maybe that's a question for you to figure out since Bonita isn't around any longer to provide answers."

His remark was a stark reminder that Bonita had been

killed last year in an early-morning pileup on Interstate 70, an accident that had killed ten people.

"I'm not going to waste time discussing our dramatic past," Canyon interrupted her thoughts to say. "What I am going to discuss is my son…a son I didn't know I had, dammit. And if you want to go sleep in a hotel room tonight without all the facts about who's trying to scare you enough to follow you home and then do this," he said, gesturing to the mess in her kitchen, "then go right ahead. But my son won't be going with you."

"Who the hell do you think you are telling me where *my* son won't be going?" she asked, taking a step closer and getting in his face.

"His father. And I think once you put your misplaced hatred for me aside, you'll agree that both of you going to Westmoreland Country would be the best thing. Would you feel safe living here?"

She tempered her anger somewhat as she took in his words. "I said I would go to a hotel."

"And what if the person finds out where you're staying? You still don't know why you're being targeted. Hell, you don't even know if it's a man or a woman. I'd think you would care about Beau's life even if you want to take chances with your own."

Keisha nibbled her bottom lip. Was Canyon deliberately trying to put the fear of God in her? She drew in a deep breath and glanced around. All it took was one look at her kitchen and the memory of the condition of the other rooms in her house. Canyon was right. Until she found out who'd done this and who had been following her earlier that day, she needed to do everything she could to keep Beau safe. And he would be safe with Canyon.

But what about her? She knew Canyon would never hurt her physically, but what about emotionally? It seemed he was still proclaiming his innocence as if she was supposed to believe him. She knew what she'd seen that night.

Keisha remembered Bonita's tearful admission that she and Canyon hadn't meant to sleep together. It had just happened. Bonita had gone to Keisha's place looking for her friend after a tiff she'd had with Grant, only to discover that Keisha hadn't yet returned from her out-of-town trip.

Bonita had been upset and to calm her down Canyon had given her something to drink, which he'd shared with her. They'd both drunk themselves silly and the next thing Bonita knew they were having sex on the floor in the living room. Canyon had taken a shower afterward and had asked Bonita to wait for him in bed.

And that was when Keisha had returned unexpectedly to find Bonita naked in bed and Canyon walking out of the bathroom wearing a towel around his middle.

Oh, he had pretended to be just as shocked as she'd been to see a naked Bonita, but Keisha hadn't bought his story then and she wasn't buying it now. There had been two empty wineglasses and Bonita's clothes had been thrown on the floor all over the place, corroborating Bonita's story.

But what if there was a smidgen of truth in what he'd said just now? What if the scene had been cunningly crafted by Bonita?

"It's getting late, Keisha, and we need to leave here," Canyon said, interrupting her thoughts.

Keisha held his gaze. Could she and Canyon spend a single day under the same roof and be civil to each other? Tomorrow was Saturday, and she had scheduled appointments to take Beau to the barbershop, do laundry, buy groceries and get her car washed. Now she would need the entire weekend to arrange the cleanup of her place. Right now she felt violated, and her main concern was keeping her son safe.

"One night," she heard herself saying. "I'll agree to stay one night." Then she thought about all that needed to be done here. "Maybe two."

Canyon frowned in exasperation. "Fine, do your two nights, but the invitation is open for as long as you need it. There's some nutcase out there and until Pete and that detective figure out what he has against you then I intend to keep you and Beau safe."

She bit her tongue to keep from telling him that neither she nor Beau needed him because that would be a lie. At this moment, with so much uncertainty in her life, for the next day…or two…she and Beau did need him.

Four

"Make yourself at home."

Keisha stepped over the threshold of Canyon's house and thought he had to be kidding. This wasn't a home, this was a friggin' castle.

It had been dark when they'd arrived but she had seen the lighted marker that denoted Westmoreland Country. And she had seen another marker that said Canyon's Bluff. Because it had been dark, she'd barely made out the massive structure until the car's headlights had shined on it. She'd sat in the car for a full minute, amazed.

He had been in the process of having the plans drawn up for the house when she'd left town. She had heard the story about how, after his parents' deaths, he and his brothers—upon reaching the age of twenty-five—inherited one hundred acres of land each…all except for Dillon. Since Dillon was the oldest, he had inherited the family home and the three hundred acres it sat on.

Canyon and several of his brothers had been perfectly content living in the main house with Dillon until Dillon had married. That was when all the brothers had decided to build their own places. Canyon hadn't been in any hurry at first. When he'd moved from Dillon's home, he and his brother Stern moved in with their brother Jason, who'd had plenty of room. Eventually, Canyon had moved in with her.

"So what do you think, Keisha?"

She glanced over at him. He was holding a sleeping Beau in his arms while standing in the middle of what she figured was his living room, although it was three times the size of hers. "Can I ask you something, Canyon?"

"What?"

"Why would a single man need such a large place?"

When he smiled she felt a stirring in her belly. "At the time, I didn't think of needs, just wants. Four of my brothers and I were building our homes practically at the same time, and we all wanted something different and unique. You think this place is big, you ought to see Micah's Manor, Derringer's Dungeon, Riley's Station, Stern's Stronghold and Zane's Hideout."

She couldn't help grinning. "I gather all of your places have unique names."

"Yes. It was Bailey's idea."

"I think the names are cute," she said, reaching for Beau.

"Whatever," he said, handing their dozing son to her.

"Those were some pretty nice neighbors to take care of him like they did."

Keisha agreed. "Yes, and I appreciate them." Janice and Everett Miles were super. Not only had they fed Beau, but they'd given him a bath and put him in a pair of the twins' pajamas. Now she held her sleeping child in her arms as she looked around a house that was too large for one person. And it was decorated for a king…and a queen. The furniture was expensive and the decor perfect.

"You must have paid a lot in decorating costs," she said.

Canyon, who was moving around turning on lights, looked over his shoulder at her and chuckled. "I wish I could say my cousin Gemma came cheap but she didn't. She made plenty of money off her brothers and cousins and wasn't guilty about doing so."

"She did a great job."

"We got what we paid for. And if you ask me, we even paid for what we didn't get. I think she deliberately overcharged us because she figured she could get away with it."

Canyon's gruffness wasn't fooling Keisha one bit since she heard the fondness in his voice. That was one thing she'd always admired about him and his family—their closeness. He had told her all about his family, and it had been her choice not to get to know them better. While Canyon had been great company, and the sex had been off the charts, she hadn't thought their relationship would last. Initially, she'd thought their physical relationship was all she'd wanted or needed.

But Canyon had had a way of growing on her, and it had seemed she had started growing on him, as well. Within six months, she had invited him to move in with her. While living together they'd gotten along fabulously and things had been going really well…until the night he'd betrayed her.

"My guest rooms are furnished but with no kiddie beds," he said, interrupting her thoughts.

"No problem, he can sleep with me."

Canyon nodded. "Okay. Right this way."

There were two spiral staircases. He moved up one and she followed, thinking his house looked even more impressive when seen from the stairs. High ceilings, crown moldings, colorful walls, hardwood and tile floors as well as intricate lighting. Everything served the purpose of complimenting the grace and style of the house. Definitely not anything a man would have had a hand in.

"Unfortunately, my place isn't childproof either."

She didn't say anything. It didn't matter since she and Beau wouldn't be staying here that long anyway. When they reached the next floor he moved into a hallway that seemed to branch out in three directions. Even this area was beautifully decorated and a huge light fixture hung from the ceiling.

He moved down a corridor containing three bedrooms. Opening the door to one of the rooms, he stood back for her to enter. This guest room, she thought, was simply stunning. There was no other word for it.

"This is the blue room," he said.

She could see why. The walls were painted sky-blue with white billowy curtains around the windows. Plaid blue-and-white coverings were on the king-size bed. A white leather love seat was on one side of the room and two beautiful white ceramic lamps sat on nightstands on either side of the bed.

"It's pretty," she said.

"Thanks."

She walked across the white marble tile to the bed, pushed back the covers and placed Beau in the center. She glanced down at their son who looked so peaceful while sleeping. Little did he know that his mother's world had just gone topsy-turvy.

"I used to do that."

She nearly jumped. She hadn't known Canyon had followed her over to the bed. "What?"

"Sleep curled up with my face resting on my hands."

She smiled. "And he makes those sounds in his sleep like you used to do."

She watched Canyon's brow rise. His eyes, normally so dark and intense, seemed even more so in the bedroom's low light. "What sounds?"

Those sounds you used to make that turned me on whenever I woke up to hear them, she thought. *Not a snore— more of a groan, as if you were having some hell of a dream.*

"So, what sounds?" he asked again.

"Not important," she said, rubbing the back of her neck. This was not how she'd planned to kick off her busy weekend. With everything she'd had planned to do Saturday and Sunday, tonight she'd hoped to curl up on her sofa with a bowl of popcorn and a movie after putting Beau to bed. Instead she was here, at the home of the one man she didn't want to deal with again.

Yes, she'd run into him occasionally since returning to Denver. Her law firm represented several of his company's clients, and she would admit that the first time they'd sat across from each other as opposing council in a legal proceeding had been difficult.

All she could think about that day, and the ones that followed, had been his betrayal. So when he'd approached her, asking if she would join him for dinner so they could talk through their issues, she had turned him down. After that it had seemed that the more she turned him down the more persistent he got. And to think he'd assumed he could follow her home to force a conversation with her!

But now she would admit she was glad he had been there when she'd walked into the house and found her home in shambles. His take-charge attitude had helped when she'd become too emotional to think straight.

"Do you think he will fall out of the bed?"

Keisha chuckled softly. "No. He's out for the night. And he's not a wanderer so don't worry about him tumbling down the stairs during the night either."

"Good, because if you're up for it, we need to go downstairs and talk."

She appreciated that he was giving her the option to say no. But she knew they needed to talk, and she wanted to get it over with. "Okay," she said, turning around.

He was standing too close, and as she looked up into his face lust shot through her. She wasn't surprised. Canyon had that effect on women. It had been that way for her the day they'd met in the courthouse lunchroom. And it had been that way a month later when she'd attended a meeting regarding a land dispute with his company. Every time Canyon glanced across the table at her she felt her insides sizzle.

"I'll need to use the ladies' room first," she said, rubbing her hands down the sides of her skirt.

"Every bedroom has a private bath. I'll see you downstairs in a few." He then turned and walked out of the room, pulling the door closed behind him.

She let out a deep breath when she heard his footsteps move down the stairs. When she'd made the decision not to tell Canyon about Beau she had been pretty comfortable with it. But she had a feeling that when Canyon finished with her she was going to wish she had decided differently.

Canyon stood at the window in his living room and looked out. It was dark, but he didn't need to see to know what was out there: the one hundred acres he had inherited.

From the time he'd been a kid, he'd known he wanted to claim this spot, the one with a perfect view of Whisper Creek Canyon. He didn't have to be on Gemma's Lake—the one named after his grandmother—or any of the other lakes and streams in Westmoreland Country. Nor did he have to be close to the valleys and meadows. This was where he wanted to be.

He recalled those times when he would go hunting with his father, uncle, brothers and cousins. They would ride their horses here on this land and then camp out near the canyon. When everyone would fall asleep he would stay awake, wide-eyed while he stared up at the stars. He was convinced only special stars shone on this spot. And they were *his* stars. Over the years, whenever he was bothered by anything, all he had to do was stare up at them to find the answers he needed.

It was here where he had escaped almost twenty years ago after finding out that his parents and uncle and aunt had died in a plane crash. And it was here where he'd come while in college when he'd made the decision to change his major from medicine to law.

He'd thought he had wanted to follow in his brother Micah's footsteps and become a doctor, but after two years of medical school he'd known he had made a mistake. He'd been torn about what to do.

Dillon had sensed something was bothering him that week when he'd come home for spring break. And it had been Dillon who'd suggested Canyon take time away from school and come home to seek the answers he needed. So Canyon had taken a semester off.

For those four months, he had crashed with his brother Riley and had spent his days either helping Ramsey with the sheep or Zane, Derringer and Jason with the horses. Then, on the weekends, he'd camped out here, on this land.

When it was time for the next semester to start, he'd made his decision to switch from medical school to law school with his family's blessings. Although his family got mad at each other sometimes, whenever it came to major issues they stuck together and supported each other.

He took another deep breath as he recalled another decision he had made here on this spot under the stars. It had been the decision to ask Keisha to marry him. One evening while she was out of town on business, he had come here. He'd already decided to build a house on this land and had been gathering ideas for what kind of home he wanted to build and exactly where he wanted the structure to face. Then, out of the clear blue sky, a voice inside his head had said, *Keisha will be the woman to live here with you.*

He really hadn't been shocked or surprised by that revelation since he'd never had issues about falling in love like some of his cousins and brothers had. He didn't have a fear of losing someone the same way he'd lost his folks. His only reason for taking his time about getting serious with a woman was that he enjoyed being single and hadn't been ready to settle down. He'd figured that one day he would meet that special person, fall in love and marry. He was fine with that idea. He just hadn't figured it would happen so soon.

He had taken a horse and ridden down into the canyon, camping out that night on this land. He'd looked up at the stars and within minutes he'd known.

He could hardly wait for Keisha to return. He hadn't been expecting her for another two days. But she'd come home early, found Bonita in her bed and assumed the worst. And Bonita had intentionally led her to believe a lie.

That angered him more than anything else about the situation because the woman had never done anything to rectify the situation. Keisha had been her friend but Bonita had lied to her. Canyon never knew what the woman's true motive had been.

Canyon's thoughts returned to the present when he

heard the sound of Keisha coming down the stairs. He turned around and moved toward her, pausing briefly to pick up the wineglass off the table where he'd placed it moments ago. "Here, I think you need this," he said, handing the glass of wine to her.

She accepted it and took a sip. He could tell from the smile on her face that she appreciated the taste. "This is good. Where did you get it?"

"My cousin Spencer and his wife own a vineyard in California's wine country. Russell Vineyard has been in Chardonnay's family for years and—"

"Chardonnay?"

"Yes, that's Spencer's wife."

"Her family owned a vineyard and named her Chardonnay?"

Canyon chuckled. "Yes, they did. I guess it's no different than my parents naming me Canyon after what they conceived on a pretty nice vacation."

He paused a moment and then asked, "How did you come up with the name Beau?"

He watched as she slid down to sit on the steps. "You don't have to sit down there when I have a perfectly good sofa," he added.

She shook her head. "No, I'm fine." She took another sip of her wine and then said, "Beau's full name is Beaumont. He was named after my uncle…my mom's only brother who died when I was a little girl. Mom and Uncle Beau were close and when I hadn't decided on a name, she asked if I would name Beau after her brother. So I did."

Canyon leaned against the staircase. "When did you find out you were pregnant?"

She took another sip of wine before glancing up at him. "I was already late when I left for Tampa but while I was there I took a pregnancy test." She paused. "The reason I came back to town early was to tell you. It was something I figured was too important to tell you over the phone. But then I found you with Bonita."

Canyon's stomach clenched in anger. Up until that moment he'd convinced himself that no matter the circumstances, he and Keisha could talk things out in a rational manner. But now, after hearing the truth from her—that she'd known she was pregnant before leaving town and had allowed her distrust to keep her from telling him he was going to be a father—was too much. He couldn't hold back his anger.

"Please come with me. I don't want to wake Beau."

Keisha followed. She'd known from the anger she heard in his voice that her words had infuriated him. It was best for them to have it out now, to get it over with. He led her through his dining room into the kitchen and she stopped in the doorway. Even the kitchen was huge and spacious. Since she knew Canyon wasn't any more of a whiz in the kitchen than she was, that meant this kitchen—with all its sterling-silver appliances, rich dark oak cabinets and beautiful granite countertops—was only a showplace.

He pulled out two chairs and remained standing as if expecting her to sit in one. She'd rather stand, but changed her mind when his glare deepened. He watched as she moved from the doorway to cross the kitchen and sit at the table. Once she sat down he claimed his seat, as well. She looked over at him and lifted her chin. "Are there any more questions, Canyon?"

She almost saw steam come from his nostrils. "You know damn well there are."

And, as if he was trying to rein in his anger, he didn't say anything for a moment. "I'm not going to restate my innocence as to what happened that night since you choose

to believe a lie. And to be quite frank, I don't care anymore what you think. Because if you can believe I did what
you've accused me of doing that means you didn't deserve
my love. I refuse to feel bad about what happened."

His words, spoken in barely contained rage, caused her
to flinch. Not because of the harshness of his tone but
because of what he was saying. Her gut clenched as his
meaning sank in. Uncertainty flowed through her. What
if she had been wrong? What if Bonita had lied? What if
he was innocent of what she'd accused him of?

She hesitated, not wanting to consider that possibility.
Everything about Bonita's story had added up. But still,
what if…

"You hated me so much that you felt I didn't need to
know I had a child?" he asked, interrupting her thoughts.

She felt the tension growing between them. "We were
no longer together and…"

When her words trailed off he lifted a brow. "And
what?"

"And after a while, I figured if I told you I was pregnant, you might question whether or not Beau was yours."

Canyon stared at her for a long moment without saying anything, but she saw the fury building in the gaze
holding hers hostage. "That's bull and you know it," he
finally said with a degree of steel in his voice that had her
shifting in her seat. "There was no reason for me to assume your baby wasn't mine. Unlike you, I trusted you.
Unconditionally. Your excuse is unacceptable, Keisha.
And what's really unacceptable is that you've been back
in Denver for ten months and you've seen me a number of
times yet you never told me I had a son. Didn't you think
I had a right to know?"

She decided to be honest with him. "No. What you did
was unforgivable and dissolved your rights where I or my

child was concerned. Besides, the last thing I wanted was for my pregnancy to make you feel obligated to a woman you evidently didn't love."

He leaned in closer to the table. "But I did love you. I told you as much a number of times."

She leaned closer as well, until their noses almost touched. "But then you showed me that love was a lie."

He pulled back and Keisha knew he was trying to control his anger. "You kept me from my son for two years because you didn't believe I loved you, because you believed that I betrayed you. What you've done is unforgivable. One day you're going to find out that the only lie in this whole thing is what you've believed for the past three years. You were wrong about me and when you find out the truth, I want you to think long and hard about what you did to me and to Beau."

Her chin stiffened. "Beau had me."

"And you were supposed to be both mother and father?"

"A woman does what she has to do when there isn't a man in the picture. My mom did."

"But you didn't give me a chance to be in the picture." He leaned back in his chair. "Is that what this is about, Keisha? Your father not wanting you, so you assumed I wouldn't want my child? If that's the case, I'm holding two strikes against you. One for not trusting me and another for thinking I'm the jerk your father was."

His words stung and stung hard. She slowly rose to her feet. "I made a mistake coming here tonight."

He tilted his head back to look up at her. "You've made several mistakes, Keisha, but coming here wasn't one of them. I am confident that one day you will realize you were wrong about me and wrong for keeping me away from my son." He paused. "But be forewarned, Beau and I won't be separated again."

She suddenly felt uneasy. "What do you mean?"

"Just what I said. If you try keeping my child from me again I will take you to court and fight you for custody. Full custody."

She gasped. "You would take my child from me?"

"Didn't you take him from me? You kept me from the pregnancy, from being there when he was born, from watching him take his first steps and from hearing him say his first words. You denied me my right to all those things, Keisha, so yes, I would take him from you, without blinking an eye. I have the means to do it. Two can play your games."

She released a frustrated breath. "Fighting between us isn't the answer, Canyon."

"Didn't say it was. But now you know where I stand." He got to his feet. "Detective Render called while you were upstairs. He'll be coming by tomorrow around noon to talk to you." He paused. "And Pam called."

She knew Pam was Dillon's wife. "And?"

"We're invited to breakfast at nine."

"I don't think—"

"At the moment, I really don't care what you think. It's time my family met my son."

She lifted her chin. "I'll go, but I won't pretend."

His gaze turned to stone but his tone was dangerously calm when he said, "Pretend what? We're in love? That we're a family? That you don't hate my guts for thinking I betrayed you, to the point where you kept my son from me for two years? No, Keisha, the last thing I want you to do is pretend you feel anything for me, because I sure as hell won't be pretending I feel anything for you."

Keisha swallowed hard as her heart pounded in her chest. In other words, even his family would know how much he despised her. "Fine," she said in a shaky breath.

"It's late, and I want to go to bed, so if you'll please grab those things out of the car I'd appreciate it."

She hadn't wanted to pack any of her things to bring with her. Her skin crawled every time she imagined anyone touching her belongings before tossing them out of the drawers and closets. Canyon had made a pit stop at a Target where she'd rushed in to grab some toiletries and an outfit for tomorrow and something to sleep in. Luckily, she kept extra clothes for Beau in a bag in her car's trunk in case of emergencies.

She would go shopping for him tomorrow before leaving for the hotel. And there was no doubt in her mind that after she talked to Detective Render she would check into a hotel.

There was no way she could stay here with Canyon another night.

An hour or so later Canyon went up to bed but he couldn't sleep. Anger kept him awake. It was fueling his mind and riling him to a degree that he'd never been before. He felt enraged. Infuriated. How dare Keisha deny him so much? Her love. His son. Her faith and trust. And all because she believed another woman's lie.

He eased out of bed and tried to put a cap on his anger. He couldn't. It was too deep. Too strong. And, to his way of thinking, too justified. He knew there was only one thing that could ease his anger: gazing through his telescope.

Because of his fascination with the stars, his cousin Ian, of the Atlanta Westmorelands, had given him this beauty after discovering Canyon's captivation with the galaxy. Like him, Ian was into stars. Canyon shook his head, thinking that was truly an understatement where his cousin was concerned. Ian was not just into stars, but the entire galaxy. He graduated from Yale with a degree in physics and had worked for NASA, as well as for a research firm, and had become the captain of his own ship, all before his thirty-third birthday. Now Ian owned the Rolling Cascade, a beauty of a casino in Lake Tahoe.

Canyon looked through the telescope, searching for one star in particular. He had first seen it at the age of ten and named it Flash. Now, twenty-two years later, Flash still had a soothing effect on him, and he really needed to see Flash tonight. It took him a full half hour before he found it and relief flooded through him as he took in the beauty of the universe.

Minutes later, he was about to get back in bed when his cell phone rang. He glanced over at the clock and saw it was almost one in the morning. "Hello?"

"I was calling to see if everything is okay."

Canyon settled in bed with his back against the headboard. When his parents, aunt and uncle had died, Dillon had become guardian to everyone under eighteen. And those over eighteen had still looked to him for guidance and leadership in keeping the family together. Canyon couldn't help but recall that the twins, Adrian and Aiden, as well as Bane and Bailey, hadn't made things easy when they'd gone through those terrible teen years.

But Dillon was still the fearless leader. He was someone they could go to for advice, knowing that with his level head he would give it to them straight. He had an uncanny sense of when one of them was troubled about anything. So, in a way, this phone call wasn't a surprise.

"Yes, Dillon. Everything is okay." He paused a moment and then added, "At least for now. But seeing how Keisha and I feel about each other tomorrow is another story."

"And just how do the two of you feel about each other, Canyon?"

Canyon released a deep sigh. "She hates me, and I hate her."

"Hate is a strong word, Can. Besides, you're not capable of hating anyone. It's not in your makeup. You might not like a person but you could never truly hate anyone."

Canyon frowned. It annoyed him that his oldest brother seemed to know him better than he knew himself. "Okay, I don't hate her. But I don't like her."

"No, because you love her."

Canyon rolled his eyes. "I *used* to love her. She destroyed that love."

"By doing what?"

"Dammit, Dil, I have a son. A son I didn't know about because she kept him from me. Even after she returned to Denver and I approached her all those times...I gave her the opportunity to tell me, and she didn't. Beau is a little over two and was born just shy of eight months after Keisha left town.

"What pisses me off more than anything is that not once did she pick up a phone, send an email, find me online or send a letter to let me know about him. And to top it off she feels she was justified because I screwed around on her. She actually still believes that. And because she believes it, she feels I had no rights where he's concerned. I missed out on the first two years of his life."

Canyon paused and then asked, "Can you imagine missing out on the first two years of Denver's life?"

There was silence on the other end before Dillon said, "No, I can't."

Canyon was certain that his brother knew how he felt. But he also knew Dillon Westmoreland was, and would always be, the voice of reason—even when no one wanted him to be.

"But look at another side of things," Dillon said.

"What other side?"

"What if she'd decided not to carry your child to term?"

Canyon closed his eyes at the thought of Keisha choosing that alternative. "Then I would hate her for sure."

"So, in other words, she's dammed if she does and damned if she doesn't."

"Don't try to defend what she did, Dil," Canyon said. His annoyance was turning to anger again, anger he'd gotten under control just moments ago.

"Not defending her, Canyon. Just giving you something to think about. Keisha thought you were unfaithful. I'm sure you'd even admit things looked pretty bad. The woman was naked in bed and you were coming out of the shower practically naked. That woman played the two of you."

"Yes, but Keisha should have believed *me*."

"I'm wondering," Dillon said, as if he'd given what he was about to say some serious thought.

"Wondering what?"

"If you had come home from a trip and found a naked man in your bed, with Keisha barely wrapped in a towel, what would you think?" Then, without missing a beat, Dillon said, "Looking forward to seeing you and your family at breakfast in the morning. Good night."

His family.

"Good night, Dil." After Canyon clicked off the line, he rubbed a hand down his face. Now he would spend the night thinking about what Dillon had said.

Five

"Wake up, Mommy. Big bed."

Keisha forced open her eyes, one at a time, to find her son's face right in front of hers. She blinked and then recalled where they were and that Beau had been asleep when they'd arrived.

She pulled up in bed and tumbled him into her arms, loving the laugh she got out of him. "Good morning, Beau. Yes, this is a *big* bed."

"Not Beau's bed."

"No, not Beau's bed," she said, running her hand through the thick curls on his head. Knowing he would have another question for her, she quickly said, "Potty?"

He nodded. "Yes, Mommy. Potty."

She eased out of bed to lead him to the bathroom and watched as he looked at everything for the first time. Beau was pretty smart for his age. He mastered his words well for a two-year-old and bathroom training hadn't been the

horror story she'd heard it would be. They had just come
out of the bathroom when there was a knock on the door.
She quickly grabbed her robe off the bed before saying,
"Come in."

Canyon strolled in.

Keisha tried not doing a double take but it was hard
when Canyon Westmoreland was eye candy. Dressed in
jeans and a Western shirt, he was the epitome of a fit male
with a physique that would put most men to shame. That
body…muscled shoulders, perfects abs and broad chest…
and she of all people knew how hard that chest was since
she'd been intimately pressed against it a number of times.
The muscles of his upper thighs would tighten whenever
she gave him a—

"And how is everyone doing this morning?" he asked.

She was grateful for his intrusion into her thoughts. The
last thing she wanted to remember was any intimacy she'd
shared with him. Her gaze moved from the lower portion
of his body and traveled up to his face. He was smiling.

What on earth did he have to smile about? And why
did it appear he was in a good mood? Before going to bed
they'd had heated words, but you wouldn't know it from
the smile on his face. Then it hit her why he was acting
so nice. Beau. Canyon might not be willing to pretend for
his family, but he evidently had no problem putting on a
front for his son.

"Dad!"

Before she could stop him, Beau took off, racing across
the room and launching his little body right at Canyon.
Canyon's deep laughter filled the room as he picked up
Beau in muscled arms and lifted him high in the air. That
got a squeal of glee from Beau.

She just stood there and watched the interaction between father and son, still somewhat astonished with how

quickly Beau took to Canyon when it usually took him a while to warm up to strangers. And before yesterday, Canyon had been a stranger.

While holding Beau high over his head, Canyon glanced over at her. She saw a flash of heat pass through his eyes and was convinced it had nothing to do with anger. In fact, she was so sure that she tightened her robe around her.

"How is everyone doing this morning?" he repeated when the only sound in the room was Beau's laughter.

Heat stung her face at the thought that he'd caught her staring. "We're fine. You're up early."

"Breakfast at the main house, remember?" he said, lowering Beau to the floor. "You haven't changed your mind about going, have you?"

As if he'd given her a choice. "No. You said nine and it's barely seven."

"I know. I got up at five and worked out some. Now I'm about to go horseback riding in the canyon, which is something I do every Saturday morning."

"Big bed, Dad."

Canyon laughed at how wide Beau had stretched out his arms.

"Mine is bigger," he said to his son, extending his arms out wider.

Beau's eyes widened. "Bigger?"

Canyon smiled. "Yes, bigger." He then glanced over at Keisha. "I'll leave you two to get dressed and will be back in an hour to give you a tour of my home."

"That's not necessary," she said.

"Yes, it is. Beau will be spending a lot of time here with me, and I want you to be comfortable that he's in a safe environment."

Tilting her head, she studied Canyon's features and saw

the same handsome man she'd always seen. But there was
a determination in his eyes that let her know that when it
came to Beau he meant what he'd said last night. He would
not let her come between him and his child again.

"I'll be ready for that tour when you get back," she said.

He arched his brow and continued to look at her as if
surprised she'd given in so easily. She was smart enough
to know which battles to fight and which ones to let go…
for now. "Come on, Beau, we need to get dressed."

"Wanna see Dad's big bed, Mommy."

She was curious about Canyon's big bed, as well. "Later,
Beau. We need to put our clothes on and get ready to go.
Your daddy is taking us somewhere."

He looked at her confused. "My daddy?"

"Yes." Keisha knew that right now, to Beau, Canyon
was Dad…as if Dad was Canyon's name and not the role
the name represented. She needed to make Beau understand. "Mommy," she said, pointing at herself. "And
Daddy," she said, pointing at Canyon.

Beau poked out his little bottom lip. "No, Mommy.
He Dad."

Keisha smiled. "Yes, and he's Daddy, too."

Beau scrunched up his face. "Daddy?"

"Yes, Daddy." She knew Beau was trying to recall all
the times he'd heard other kids use the word *daddy,* mostly
during pickup at day care or when the twins next door
talked to Everett. Beau had never been around a male
for any long period of time, and he certainly hadn't been
around one that he could call daddy. Until now.

Beau turned to Canyon and a big, wide smile spread
across his lips. "Wanna see your big bed, Daddy-Dad."

Canyon couldn't help but laugh out loud before saying. "And you will, but not now." He looked at Keisha.
"Thanks."

* * *

Canyon knew what Keisha had tried to do this morning with Beau, and he appreciated it.

After one hell of a sleepless night, he'd woken up determined to make this a good day. He would be introducing Beau to his family, and he was pretty damn excited about it.

An hour later, as Canyon returned from riding his horse, he was still filled with excitement. There was something about riding across his land and through the canyon that soothed him. Not only was it his heritage and his legacy, it was also his solace. And one day he would leave it all to his son.

Beau.

The realization that he had a son filled him in a way he hadn't thought possible. A child had never been a top priority for him. Hell, a wife hadn't either, until Keisha. But seeing Beau, holding him, touching him—that parental part of Canyon had come alive and had become so deep that he could feel it in every part of his body. He'd meant every single word he'd told Keisha last night. He didn't intend to be separated from his child ever again.

He wasn't sure how she would deal with it or how she would deal with him. That wasn't his concern. The only thing that mattered to him was building a strong relationship with his child, starting now. Today. He needed to make up for all the time he'd lost, and he refused to let her stand in his way.

He recognized the frigid looks she was prone to giving him and knew his responsive stare was just as bad. The only thing holding his temper in check whenever he thought about the two years he'd lost was to remember what Dillon had said last night. She could have made a different decision regarding Beau, but she hadn't.

He walked into his house, placed his Stetson on the hat rack and glanced up at the same time that Keisha and Beau were coming down the stairs. Beau grinned wide when he saw Canyon and was about to take off toward him, but Keisha held firm to his hand. "No, Beau. Remember. No running down the stairs."

"Yes, Mommy."

Canyon couldn't stop staring at Keisha. She had changed into a pair of jeans and a pullover blouse. To his way of thinking, she looked absolutely beautiful. He recalled yesterday when he'd seen her walk out of her office and noticed that her body had changed. Now he knew why. Because of Beau.

She'd always had a nice body, now it was even curvier. More enticing. More tempting.

He pushed those thoughts from his mind. He would not become involved with a woman who didn't trust him, and she'd proved just how much she didn't.

As soon as Beau's feet touched the floor, he took off running toward Canyon. "You know the rule, Beau," Keisha said. "No running in the house."

He stopped and looked back at Keisha. "Not my house."

Canyon had to cough to keep from laughing out loud and hung his head when Keisha shot him a warning look. "It doesn't matter, young man, whose house it is. No running in any house. Understand?"

He nodded and then walked as fast as his little legs could take him to Canyon. He reached up his arms. "Pick me up high again, Daddy-Dad."

"See what you started," Keisha said.

Canyon chuckled as he hoisted Beau up in the air, thinking that he didn't mind. In fact, he loved hearing the sound of his son's laughter. "And for the record, this is your house, too, Beau." He glanced over at Keisha with a look that dared her to refute his words.

He placed Beau on his shoulders and said, "Now for that tour I promised you."

Keisha had already seen Canyon's living and dining rooms as well as the kitchen. But he showed all of it to her again anyway. "While I'm showing you around, note if anything is a red flag where a child is concerned and let me know so I can change it."

"All right," Keisha said as he led her up the second set of spiral stairs.

This was the first house she'd seen that had two beautiful spiral staircases, but the layout didn't look odd. The two staircases appeared to join at the top, when they really did not. The effect was simply breathtaking.

With Beau still perched on his shoulder Canyon turned when they reached the landing. "This is where my suite is located as well as other rooms for my pleasure."

For his pleasure? She wondered what kind of rooms they were.

It didn't take her long to find out. She entered the first room, the one he'd called his mini-gym. His personal workout room had every piece of weight-lifting equipment imaginable. Next was a game room with a dartboard, a pool table and a big flat-screen television that seemed to be over eight feet wide.

"Nice," she said. She could envision him in both rooms after a long and tiresome day at the office. He would probably work out first, shower and then go into his game room and unwind before calling it a night.

"This way to my bedroom," he said, leading her down a spacious hall that led to massive double doors made of dark oak. When he opened the door she just stood in the doorway and stared.

"Big, big bed, Mommy."

That was an understatement. She was familiar with a queen-size bed since she had one of her own, and of course she'd seen a king-size. But this one had to be a super-duper king. "Yes, this is definitely big."

"*Big, big,* Mommy," Beau reiterated

She chuckled. "Okay, Beau. Big, big. Your daddy has a *big, big* bed."

"Let's see if it's too big for you," Canyon said, dumping Beau off his shoulders and into the center. Beau bounced up and down, laughing a few times.

"Fun, Mommy, fun. Come on bed, Mommy. Get in Daddy-Dad bed."

Keisha was certain her face tinted at the thought of her doing that. "No thanks. I'll just stand here and watch you." She didn't have to glance over at Canyon to know he was looking at her. She could feel the heat of his gaze all over.

Instead of looking at Canyon, she walked over to the huge wall-to-wall window. He had an amazing view from his bedroom, of the canyon as well as the Denver sky above it.

Her heart began pounding in her chest when she felt Canyon's heat and knew he had come to stand behind her. To take her mind off his presence, she said, "This is a beautiful view of the canyon."

"Yes, I think so, as well. That's why I designed the house this way so I could wake up to the canyon every morning."

She turned and noticed Beau still bouncing as if Canyon's bed was a trampoline. "And what about your guests? They don't have this view."

He shrugged as an impish grin touched his lips. "No,

all the guest rooms have a view of the mountains. I don't think that's so bad."

She didn't think it was so bad either. In fact, she'd liked it, and when she'd woken up this morning, she couldn't help looking out the window at the mountains while getting dressed. This house, Canyon's Bluff, could grow on a person.

"Come on, let me show you the other parts of the house." He moved away, went to the bed and caught Beau in his arms as he bounced. Canyon then left the room.

She followed, taking a quick peek into his bathroom. She shook her head. The master bath was to die for and was bigger than the living room at her house. *Her house.* She then remembered why she was here and what someone had done to her home, her sanctuary. The place where she'd always felt secure. She couldn't push away the thought that someone had intentionally taken that security from her. Like the deputy had said, whoever had trashed her home had done so to make a point. But she had no idea what it was.

Fifteen minutes later, Canyon ended his tour in the room that housed an indoor swimming pool. Like the rest of the house, the room was beautiful, and no matter what the weather was outside—even if the grounds were blanketed in snow—you could have a nice swim.

"So did you see anything?" he asked in a voice that, to her way of thinking, sounded way too sexy. They were leaving the pool room, and he took the time to lock the door behind him.

She lifted a brow. "Anything like what?"

"Anything I need to be concerned about when Beau spends the weekends."

His words reminded her that he intended to be a part of her son's life, her life, whether she wanted him to or not.

"The only thing I saw that would concern me is the pool. Beau can't swim."

He nodded as he led them back to the living room. Beau was still riding Canyon's shoulders with his legs dangling around Canyon's neck. "No problem. I intend to start teaching him how to swim next week."

Keisha bit down on her lip to keep from telling Canyon he shouldn't make assumptions. Granted, upon seeing how well Canyon and Beau were getting along, a part of her was regretting keeping them apart, but she refused to let him run roughshod over her.

She was still Beau's custodial parent…although she had placed Canyon's name as the father on the birth certificate. That had been the one concession she'd given after being hassled by her mother. Lynn had regretted not putting Kenneth Drew's name on Keisha's birth certificate. Even though Kenneth had not claimed his daughter, she was his blood nonetheless. Acknowledging that kinship would have at least given Keisha the name of the man who'd fathered her.

"If you recall, I taught you how to swim," Canyon said, putting Beau down on the floor, watching as he walked quickly over to the huge aquarium and pressed his face against it.

Keisha felt an intense pull in her stomach. Canyon would have to remind her of those lessons. It had taken triple the length of time it should have taken…not that she hadn't been an adept student. But mainly because they had spent their time exploring the numerous positions a couple could use while making love in water. To this day she would never forget those swimming lessons on one of the lakes in Westmoreland Country, and judging by the way he was looking at her, he hadn't forgotten either. Just remembering sent sensual chills through her body. Chills she didn't want to feel.

Deciding not to respond to his comment about her swimming lessons, she said, "As to the other parts of your home, I didn't notice anything since we won't be staying long. However, I would like to take a more in-depth tour later today on my own."

Being around him was unnerving her when it shouldn't. She'd accepted that the sexual chemistry was still there, even after three years, but she had expected to be able to handle it much better than she was.

"Help yourself. I want to make sure I do things right, and I want to make sure you won't be worried when he's here with me."

"But I *will* worry anyway, Canyon," she said honestly. "And when I do worry, please don't take it personally. It comes with being a mother. Now that you know about him, you'll worry, too, although you know I'm capable of taking care of him. It comes with being a father." She hesitated a moment and then added, "Although some men take that role more seriously than others." She smiled. "I even worried every day when he was with Mom. I used to call so much she would fuss at me for bothering her."

Canyon thought about what Keisha had just said. "Your mother took care of him every day while you worked?" he asked.

"For the first eight months. She took a leave from her job just to do it."

He'd never met her mother but had spoken to her once or twice on the phone when she'd called. He knew of Keisha and her mother's close relationship. He also knew Keisha had inherited her mother's independent nature. Keisha had told him the story of how her father had denied she was his child when her mother had told him about her pregnancy and how her mother had raised her alone without any involvement from him.

Canyon noticed when Keisha glanced at her watch. "I guess we need to leave if we want to—"

She stopped talking when he reached out and took her wrist in his hand and looked at the watch…remembering. "You kept it."

It was a statement more than a question and he was well aware that she knew it. He had given her the bracelet watch for her birthday a few weeks before she'd broken up with him.

"Yes, I kept it. Did you think I was going to throw it away?"

He shrugged. "That had crossed my mind."

She absently flexed her fingers and he knew she was nervous about something. "Are you nervous about Detective Render's visit later today?"

She glanced over at Beau before shifting her head back over to him. "No. That's not it."

He lifted a brow. "Then what is it?"

She nibbled on her bottom lip. "It's your family."

"What about them?"

She drew in and then released a deep breath. "You and I agreed we won't be pretending and I have a feeling they won't either."

He tilted his head. "Meaning?"

Lowering her voice so Beau wouldn't hear, she said, "You and your family are close, Canyon. You and I didn't part on the best terms, and I'm sure they know all about it. There's no doubt in my mind they'll be taken with Beau, but…"

"But what?"

"Maybe you should have found out for certain if they really want me there. I have done things they probably don't agree with. I'm sure most of them took your side about what happened. They probably figure I should have believed what you said. And that I was wrong for not telling you about Beau. Even you believe I was wrong on both counts so how can I expect them to feel any differently?"

Canyon didn't say anything for a minute. "First of all, please stop judging my family prematurely. You met most of them already—all of my brothers, except for Bane and Micah, and all of my cousins except for Gemma, since she'd already married and moved to Australia. You and I met the year after I returned home from law school, so you already know some of my brothers' and cousins' wives. You met Pam, Chloe, Lucia and Bella, because Dillon, Ramsey, Derringer and Jason had married them by the time you and I started dating."

Although she was three years younger than his thirty-two, they had finished their respective law schools at the same time, mainly because of the extra time it had required for him to change his major. He would never forget the day they'd met in the courthouse lunchroom. He had been an attorney for fewer than six months and had won his first case that day. She had won her case that day, as well. They had celebrated that night over drinks.

"My family," he continued, "will decide if they like you because of you and not because of me. They'll let our business be our business. The Westmorelands make it a point to stay out of each others' affairs." He chuckled. "The only time we didn't abide by that rule was when Derringer got involved with Lucia. She was Chloe's best friend and childhood friends with Megan and Gemma. So, unfortunately for Derringer, those of us who knew his reputation were overprotective where Lucia was concerned."

He paused. "When you and I were involved I tried to get you to spend more time with my family, but you declined all my invitations. If anything, they probably think you have something against them because you never wanted to get to know them before."

His statement sent an embarrassing tint across her cheeks. What he'd said was true. She had turned down invitations to his family's chow-downs and other little activities. But it hadn't been because she'd had anything against them.

Her grandparents didn't have any siblings and her mother had had only one brother. For that reason, the thought of a family as large as Canyon's was overwhelming to her. Luckily, he'd understood and hadn't pushed. When she'd attended that charity ball with him and finally met his family, she'd found them to be nice and very friendly. His sisters-in-law and his cousins-in-law—Pam, Chloe, Lucia and Bella—had invited her to lunch, but before she could take them up on their offer, she and Canyon had split up.

"I had planned to get to know them better," she said in her defense. "But both of us know what happened, don't we?"

The look in his eyes turned cold. "Yes, we know. You chose to believe a lie rather than the truth."

Keisha opened her mouth to give him a blistering retort, when she felt a tug on her jeans. Beau pulled on Canyon's pants, too, and then glanced up at them with big pleading brown eyes. "Bouncy bed again?"

She knew Canyon was about to give in when he reached down to pick up Beau, but Keisha knew her son's antics better than anyone. He would use those beautiful eyes to wrap a person around his finger, and he'd figured out that Canyon was an easy target.

"No, Beau," she said firmly. "No bouncy bed again."

She then switched her gaze back to Canyon. "I'm ready to go now."

Canyon nodded and, without saying anything, he led her toward the door.

"I don't believe it," Pamela Westmoreland said, staring at the little boy in Canyon's arms. She turned to her husband who was standing at her side. "Can you believe it?"

Dillon smiled. "Yes. That's how Dare and I knew we were cousins the first time we met because we looked so much alike. Strong Westmoreland genes."

Canyon chuckled. "I don't think Keisha believes us. I can't wait until she sees Denver. Where is he by the way?"

"In the back with Bailey," Dillon said, grinning. "Playing with Denver gives Bailey the excuse to act like a kid again. Come on in. Welcome to our home, Keisha."

"Thank you," Keisha said, glancing around. This was a big house, bigger than Canyon's. She knew all about the history of Dillon's home. It had been built by Canyon's great-grandfather and passed on to his grandfather who'd passed it on to his two sons. The house tripled in size when both sons, their wives and their families lived here—in what was considered the main house—in harmony. Then the sons and their wives died and as the oldest grandchild Dillon had inherited the house and the three hundred acres it sat on.

"So good seeing you again, Keisha," Pam said, giving her a hug. That was something else Keisha had tried to get used to when it came to Canyon's family. They were such a huggy group. She and her mother were close, but didn't hug as much as the Westmorelands did.

"Canyon told us what happened to your home. That's just awful. If there's anything any of us can do, please let us know."

"Thanks." Keisha felt Pam's offer was sincere, and she appreciated it. Pam Westmoreland was a beautiful woman. Keisha had thought that same thing the first time she'd seen Pam on her husband's arm at the ball. And from what Canyon had told her, Pam, a former actress who'd lived in California at one time, was perfect for his brother.

"Where are the others?" Canyon asked. "I see the cars out front."

"They're out back, as well," Dillon said. "It's such a nice day that Pam and the ladies decided to set up things outside on the patio. And speaking of cars, yours is parked in the back, Canyon."

"Thanks for handling that for me."

"No problem. Everyone expects you to be here, and I didn't mention anything about Keisha and Beau. I decided to let you handle it."

Keisha felt her stomach tighten. She could just imagine how many of Canyon's family members were here. She inwardly prepared herself for a lot of cold stares. Things would be worse when they saw Beau. He was their family, and they would probably resent her for keeping him from them.

"Jill flew in last night, and I'm excited about it," Pam said, grinning from ear to ear.

"Jillian is Pam's sister," Dillon said, chuckling. "She's twenty-four and in medical school in Louisiana, with a goal of one day becoming a neurosurgeon. She couldn't make it home for Megan's wedding, so this is the first time we've seen her this year. We're all excited she was able to get time off to come home for a few days."

Dillon led them through a huge dining room and a very spacious kitchen. Keisha recalled what Canyon had once told her. When Dillon had married Pam she had been the guardian of her three younger sisters who'd come to live with them in this house, as well. It seemed fitting that a man who'd once made it his life's mission to be responsible for his younger siblings and cousins had married a woman who'd done practically the same thing.

Keisha drew in a deep breath when they reached the sliding glass door. Outside, she saw a beautiful patio with the most gorgeous view of a huge lake. She felt Canyon slip his hand in hers and she glanced up at him. The look in his eyes was unreadable, but she figured he knew how nervous she was and he was letting her know he was there for her. His actions were confusing. He'd said he wouldn't pretend, so why was he acting as if he cared?

"Look who finally got here," Dillon said, stepping out onto the patio with Pam at his side.

Keisha watched as everyone looked over at them. Her presence garnered only a little interest. The one who really snagged everyone's attention was Beau.

"Hey, guys. Most of you know Keisha," Canyon said. "I want to introduce you to our son, Beau."

Everyone stared without saying anything. Keisha had known meeting Beau would be a surprise, but the crowd's response made her wonder why so much attention had been drawn to Beau. Were all the shocked expressions necessary?

Just then, a little boy raced across the room toward Dillon. "Daddy! Daddy! Look what Megan gave me."

Keisha glanced down at the little boy and her breath caught. Her hand flew to her chest. "My God!" she whispered in shock.

The little boy could be Beau's twin.

Six

"I tried to tell you," Canyon whispered in Keisha's ear. She felt her body tremble slightly from the heat of his breath so close to her skin.

Dillon swung his son up into his arms as pandemonium hit. Canyon's siblings and cousins rushed over to them. The ones she had met before gave her hugs and told her it was good seeing her again. She tried to keep surprise out of her features.

They cooed and aahed over Beau, who seemed to enjoy getting so much attention. No one questioned why they were just now meeting him for the first time. Keisha figured they were staying out of Canyon's business because they knew he would handle it.

"How old is he?" Bailey asked. She was the one holding Beau and didn't seem inclined to relinquish him.

"He's a little over two."

Bailey smiled as she looked back and forth between

Beau and Denver. "Denver is almost four. Except for their size, they have the same facial features. That's absolutely incredible."

Keisha thought it was pretty incredible, as well. If Denver wasn't taller and almost two years older, the little boys could pass for twins. And speaking of twins...

The Westmoreland twins stood in front of her, smiling, and she couldn't help but smile back. Identical twins. Even down to their handsome grins. She couldn't forget the identity trick they'd played on her the night she had met them.

"Aiden and Adrian." She lifted a brow then looked from one to the other. "Or is it Adrian and Aiden."

Their identical smiles widened. "We'll never tell," one of them said.

"Okay, guys, you've forced my hand now I'm forcing yours." She reached out and took one of their right hands and turned it over so that it was palm up. She nodded and then glanced back up at the man whose hand she held. "You're Adrian."

Both men shifted their gazes from her to Canyon and Aiden said accusingly, "You told."

Canyon shrugged, and Keisha couldn't help but grin. Yes, Canyon had told her that the only way to tell the two apart was by the tiny scar in the palm of Adrian's right hand just under his thumb. It had been a childhood injury caused by falling out of a tree.

"Move over guys, Keisha needs to come with us so we can girl talk," Ramsey's wife, Chloe, said, taking Beau from Bailey. Bailey then reached for Denver and when the two women stood side by side with both boys everyone just shook their heads. The two boys seemed as fascinated with each other as much as everyone was fascinated with them.

"Now Denver has a playmate he can do guy stuff with," Dillon said, grinning. "Susan is getting too prissy for him."

Susan was Ramsey and Chloe's daughter who was a few months younger than Denver.

"I hope when they grow older they don't play those crazy games and go around tricking people like Aiden and Adrian used to do," Megan said, laughing.

"You mean those games they still like to play?" Riley Westmoreland said as he came to join them. "Keisha, I'd like you to meet my fiancée, Alpha Blake."

Instead of extending her hand, Alpha reached out and gave Keisha a hug. "Congratulations, and nice meeting you."

"Same here."

"Think I can have my son back now?" Canyon asked, reaching for Beau.

"I guess," Chloe said, smiling, handing Beau to Canyon.

With a huge grin on his face, Beau reached out eagerly to go to Canyon. "Daddy-Dad."

Canyon's brother Jason raised a brow. "Daddy-Dad?"

Canyon chuckled as he perched Beau on his shoulder. "It's a long story." He then glanced around and asked, "Where's Zane?"

Trying to keep a straight face, Riley said, "I guess he and Channing decided to sleep in this morning. We expect them later."

Canyon nodded. He then shifted his gaze to where the Westmoreland women had led Keisha off to a section of the patio. He knew how reserved Keisha was with new people and inwardly smiled. She was going to find out that when it came to the Westmorelands, the word *reserved* wasn't in their vocabulary.

"Hey, Can. You okay?" Stern asked his brother when he followed Canyon's gaze over to Keisha.

"Yes, I'm okay. Why wouldn't I be?"

Stern shrugged. "No reason. Just asking." He paused. "She looks good."

Canyon switched his gaze off Keisha and onto his brother. "I see your eyesight is still good. But I suggest you check out somebody else."

Stern laughed. "Getting testy, aren't we?"

Canyon shifted Beau in his arms, refusing to be baited. At that moment, Canyon's cousin Zane and his fiancée, Channing Hastings, arrived and stepped out onto the patio. Everyone greeted the couple and Channing couldn't resist holding Beau. She left to join the ladies with Beau in her arms. It was then that Zane pulled Canyon aside.

"I see you handled your business without my help," Zane said, glancing over at Keisha.

Canyon rolled his eyes. He had called Zane a few weeks ago when he'd gotten fed up with Keisha trying to avoid him. That was when he'd come up with the plan for following her home. "Yes, but it's not what you think."

"Well, I've got a feeling you're going to find out like I did that…once your woman, always your woman."

Canyon was about to tell Zane how wrong he was when Zane walked off to talk to Ramsey and Dillon. Feeling frustrated, Canyon moved across the patio to get his son, wanting to spend as much time with him as he could.

Despite Keisha's apprehensions about sharing an amicable relationship with the women surrounding her, she couldn't help it. They were so outgoing, friendly and personable that she found it hard to resist their camaraderie. It had been the same way that night at the ball.

She had fond memories of that night even though she had been a little overwhelmed by Canyon's family. He'd introduced her to not only the ones living in Denver, but also the ones living in Atlanta, Montana and Texas. The one thing she would always remember about that night was how easily they had accepted her. It was as if they'd made up their minds. If Canyon had brought her with him then that meant something. Too bad that she'd believed the same thing only to find out months later just how wrong her assumption had been.

She glanced across the patio to the yard where Canyon was helping Beau go up and down a kiddie sliding board that was part of a cedar swing set. There was also a sandbox, an outdoor playhouse and several other pieces of playground equipment in a play area separated from the lake by a high fence.

She could hear Beau's laughter and knew he was having the time of his life. As if he felt someone looking at him, Canyon glanced over at her. His dark gaze was neither friendly nor sensual as he stared back. But that didn't stop the heat slowly inching across her skin. The attraction that was still there between them was frustrating. She was certain he didn't like it any more than she did.

Holding back a sigh, she broke eye contact with him to watch the women sitting around her. In addition to Dillon's wife, Pam, Ramsey's wife, Chloe, and Riley's fiancée, Alpha, there were also Kalina, who was married to Canyon's brother Micah; Canyon's cousin Megan, who'd gotten married a couple of months ago; Lucia, who was married to his cousin Derringer; and Bella, who was married to his brother Jason. And then there was Channing Hastings. From what Keisha had gathered, Channing and Zane had broken up a while ago but had patched things up and were now back together.

Also included in the mix were Pam's three gorgeous sisters. Jillian was twenty-four; Paige was twenty-two, had recently graduated with a degree from UCLA and was living in Los Angeles determined to follow in her big sister's footsteps and become an actress; and Nadia, who was in her second year of college at the University of Wyoming. It was easy to see that Pam adored her younger sisters and they adored her.

Keisha was drawn back into the conversation among the women. Jillian was talking about how hard medical school was and it was then that Keisha noticed Bailey staring at her.

While the other women would allow her and Canyon to deal with their issues in their own way, without taking any sides, she had a feeling Bailey wasn't prone to doing that. The youngest Westmoreland had immediately been taken with Beau and was probably resenting the fact that this was the first time any of them had seen him. Keisha wondered if the others felt that way but were just doing a better job of hiding their true feelings than Bailey.

And then, as if Pam had somehow picked up on the question floating through Keisha's mind, she reached out, touched her hand, smiled and said, "We're glad to have you as part of the family, Keisha."

Keisha swallowed hard. Although she appreciated Pam's words, Keisha knew she needed to set the record straight. "But I'm not part of the family. Canyon and I aren't together that way."

Pam waved off her words. "Beau is a Westmoreland and you're Beau's mother, so that makes you part of the family."

Keisha had news for her. Things didn't work out that way, and no doubt Canyon would make certain they didn't. Deciding not to disagree with Pam for now, Keisha took another sip of her orange juice.

Jillian excused herself to go to the ladies' room and Nadia stood to take Pamela's other son, seven-month-old Dade, out of Pam's arms. Paige gathered the other young ones together and herded them to the kiddie playground.

Keisha had been introduced to all the kids and it seemed a number of them were close to Beau's age. Ramsey and Chloe had three-and-a-half-year-old Susan, as well as two-year-old Rembrandt. Micah and Kalina had two-year-old Macon and Kalina was pregnant again with a girl. Derringer and Lucia had a two-year-old son named Ringo; and Jason and Bella had two-year-old twin daughters—Faith and Hope—and Bella mentioned that she and Jason wanted at least two more kids. Keisha felt good knowing that during those weekends Beau would spend with Canyon, he would have plenty of cousins to romp around with.

"Isn't Canyon's home just gorgeous?" Bailey asked.

Keisha wondered if anyone else had picked up on Bailey's snide question. Bailey was no doubt trying to make a point while fishing for information; specifically, whether or not Keisha had spent the night in Canyon's home. Although the others were too polite to ask, no doubt they were wondering how Canyon had found out about Beau and what status she held in Canyon's life.

Keisha decided that whatever information they got about Beau, Canyon would give them himself. However, she had no problem letting them know—once again—that she and Canyon weren't sharing that kind of relationship. She didn't have any status in Canyon's life.

She held Bailey's gaze. "Yes, Canyon has a gorgeous home, and I appreciate him letting me stay there for the night considering what happened to mine."

Chloe arched her brow. "What happened to yours?"

Keisha frowned slightly. Had Canyon not told his family about why she had stayed with him? "My house got trashed."

"What!"

The single word of shocked surprise spouted simultaneously from every women sitting around her. "Yes, it got trashed." She then told them what had happened from the time she'd left work yesterday up to now.

"And the police have no idea who was following you or who trashed your house?" Lucia asked, clearly outraged.

"So far, no," Keisha said. Talking about it made her angry once again at what had happened. "A Detective Render is meeting me at Canyon's home at noon to go over everything and to ask more questions."

"I've met Ervin Render before," Megan said. "He's loaned his expertise to a couple of cases Rico has worked on. Rico says he's good." Rico Claiborne was Megan's husband and a private investigator.

"I'm glad to hear that. I plan to stay in a hotel tonight, and I want to feel safe doing so."

"Maybe you shouldn't say in a hotel, Keisha," Bella said. "At least not until they find out who trashed your house."

"They didn't take anything of value?" Bailey asked, as if to make sure she'd heard correctly.

Keisha shook her head. "No, they didn't. Not my jewelry, my coin collection or anything. It's pretty darn obvious whoever did it wants to scare me."

There, she'd said it herself. The police deputy had said the same thing but this was the first time she'd said the truth out loud. Saying it sent a cold chill through her body. She couldn't think of one reason why anyone would want to do that. But evidently someone did.

Leaving Beau in the care of Paige, who had gathered the kids together to play several games, Canyon went into the kitchen and grabbed a beer out of Dillon's refrigerator. It was early, but he needed something stronger than orange juice to calm his libido.

Every time he glanced over to where Keisha was sitting

on the patio with the Westmoreland women, he couldn't stop his body from revving up into a state of sexual desire. Why did she have to look so damn good? And why did his heart pound like crazy in his chest each and every time she opened her mouth to talk? More than once, he'd been tempted to leave the kids' play area, cross the yard and pull her into his arms for a kiss. He could just imagine tangling his tongue with hers like they did in the good old days.

Deciding to make a pit stop at the bathroom before grabbing his beer, he rounded the corner and slowed when he recognized the voices in the hallway. He was about to greet the two people talking, when the words being spoken between them made him stop.

Aiden released a deep sigh and tipped Jillian's chin up so that she was staring into the depths of his dark eyes. "It's time we tell them, Jill. I don't like sneaking around."

"I don't like sneaking around either, but you promised we would wait until I finished medical school. You said you understood," she murmured softly.

"I did at the time, but now I don't anymore. I think Dillon and Pam will be okay to know that we've fallen in love."

"But you don't know that for certain. As far as they're concerned we're family. Your cousin married my sister, and that makes us—"

"Legally no kin," Aiden said in a voice tinged with frustration.

"But Dillon tells me, Nadia and Paige all the time that we're part of the Westmoreland family."

"Because he married your sister. So to him, and to all of us, you are. But you're not a blood relative, and I've never thought of you as anything other than the woman I love and want. Nothing about that is going to change, Jill."

"Oh, Aiden, then promise me you'll wait a little bit longer. I don't want to cause a rift within the family."

"You won't."

"I might, and I don't want to take that chance," she said, fighting back a sob. "Please understand."

"Don't cry, baby. I'll wait a little while longer because you're worth waiting for. Always have been."

"Oh, Aiden."

He pressed a light kiss to her lips but a fierce longing and desire had him pulling her into his arms and taking her mouth with a hunger that sent a rush of need through him.

When Aiden lifted his head, he stared deep into Jillian's eyes for a long moment before lowering his mouth to hers once again…

"Damn," Canyon muttered under his breath as he quietly backed up.

When had this started? Hell. He didn't want to be around when Dillon and Pam found out. Dillon probably wouldn't have much to say because he'd gotten used to Bane and Crystal sneaking around. But Canyon wasn't so sure how Pam would take the news.

Jillian had been seventeen when Dillon married Pam and brought her and her sisters to Westmoreland Country. Canyon, the twins and Stern had mostly been away at college, and Bane had already left for the navy. So when had Jillian and Aiden gotten together? Over the holidays? During spring breaks? It sounded serious. He hoped so, for Aiden's sake. Everyone knew how protective Pam was of her three sisters, and Aiden had always had a reputation for playing women. If Pam thought some funny business had been going on under her nose all this time and that Aiden didn't mean Jillian any good, then there would be hell to pay.

Maybe Canyon ought to talk to Aiden. Then, on second thought, maybe he should tend to his own business, which was pretty messed up at the moment. He had a son he'd just found out about and a former lover staying at his house who still hated his guts.

His plate was full, and he didn't need anyone else's problems to add to it. Opening the French doors, he stepped back onto the patio and looked to where Keisha was still sitting and talking to the women in his family. He wasn't sure what they were talking about, but from their expressions, the conversation looked serious.

He glanced at his watch. It was almost eleven, and Detective Render was supposed to be at his place to question Keisha at noon. He moved to the playground to get Beau. After thanking Paige for entertaining his son and letting Dillon know he was on his way out, Canyon walked to where Keisha was sitting.

"I hate to break up this little party but Keisha, Beau and I have to leave," Canyon said.

Keisha glanced up at Canyon. He had Beau in his arms and stood tall with his Stetson on his head, which Beau seemed to find fascinating. "All right," she said, standing.

"Don't let her stay at a hotel tonight Canyon." To Keisha's surprise, that directive had come from Bailey.

"I won't."

Keisha frowned at Canyon who merely stared back at her. He'd said it like he could stop her from leaving his home if that was what she wanted to do. She bit her lip to keep from setting him straight in front of his family.

"I think we should go shopping," Megan said quickly, as if that was the answer for anything and everything.

When everyone stared at Megan, she shrugged and said, "I figure you didn't bring a lot of your things over, and even if the detective says it's okay for you to return home, it's going to take a while to clean up the mess…which we'll all pitch in and help you do, of course. But regardless, Keisha, you're going to need a few items now."

"Whether you stay at Canyon's place or a hotel," Bella added, smiling.

"We can go after church," Kalina said excitedly, as if the thought of going shopping had stirred her blood. "I need to pick up some more maternity outfits anyway."

"Going shopping is a great idea," Lucia piped in to say.

Keisha saw she was outnumbered but decided not to make any promises. "We'll see. Check with me tomorrow." She then bid everyone goodbye as Canyon led her off the patio.

Seven

Keisha checked her watch after putting Beau to bed for his nap. Detective Render would be arriving in a few minutes and since she hadn't heard anything from Pete, she could only assume the police didn't have any answers for her yet.

Canyon hadn't had much to say on the drive back home from Dillon's place. No comments and no questions. It was as if he had a lot on his mind or was deliberately ignoring her. She wished she could do the same and ignore him, but there was just something about a man with so much testosterone. He was sexy without even trying to be and her body responded.

Whenever she'd focused on his hands, which had gripped the steering wheel, she couldn't help but remember how those same hands had stroked her body, had fondled her and had masterfully caressed her breasts. She'd sat there, crossing her legs and then uncrossing them a number of times before they'd arrived at Canyon's Bluff. If he'd found her fidgeting in her seat unusual, he made no mention of it.

After freshening up in the bathroom for her meeting with Detective Render, she glanced over at Beau and saw he was still sleeping peacefully. Keisha couldn't help but smile when she thought about all the fun Beau had had today with his cousins. He'd barely made it back here before falling asleep.

And she would have to admit that he wasn't the only one who'd had a good time. Considering her and Canyon's strained relationship, she had been surprised by just how warm and fuzzy Canyon's family had made her feel. She hadn't expected their acceptance and although Canyon had tried to assure her that his family wouldn't be rude because of what was going on with them, she hadn't believed it. Everyone had gone out of their way to be kind to her.

The ladies had even offered to go shopping with her, although she didn't intend to take them up on the offer. When Beau woke up in an hour, she would pack up the things she'd brought here and check in to a hotel. She would call Mr. Spivey on Monday morning to let him know what had happened and ask for a few days off to return some order to her home. Instead of accepting Canyon's family's offer to assist her with that as well, she would hire someone from a cleaning company.

Although Bailey hadn't come across as warm and fuzzy as all the others, she had shown concern about Keisha staying at a hotel. But then, she could have been more concerned for Beau's welfare than Keisha's.

Shrugging and deciding not to dwell on it any longer, Keisha moved toward the window to appreciate the beautiful view of the mountains. Canyon's bedroom view might be of the canyon, but she thought this view was just as

breathtaking. A movement made Keisha glance down into
Canyon's yard. She saw him, near the barn, bending down
while cleaning his saddle. In addition to teaching her to
swim, he'd taught her to ride a horse. Those were two
things he intended to teach their son to do.

And then, as if Canyon had radar where she was concerned, he glanced up to the window and snagged her
gaze. Her breath caught. She could still see the anger in
the dark depths but now she saw something else. She felt
it. In every part of her body.

Canyon's look always unnerved her, which was why she
never maintained eye contact with him for any length of
time…especially when they were sitting across the table
from each other during client negotiations. So far they'd
never had to face each other in a court of law. And she
hoped that time never came.

She drew in a deep breath as his gaze continued to hold
hers like a magnet. Tight. Fixed. Unyielding. It was eerie,
stimulating and stirring, in a sensual kind of way—all at
the same time. Without breaking eye contact, he straight-
ened. *Tall, dark and too handsome for his own good.*

There was such strength and masculinity in his tall form
that her heartbeat increased and her nipples transformed
to hardened nubs.

She recalled how he used to unbutton her blouse, undo
the front clasp to her bra and suck her nipples between
his lips.

Geez. Why were all her memories of him so sexual?

Because even though they had enjoyed each other out
of bed, their relationship had been sexual. And boy had
she enjoyed their bed time. Canyon could stroke her into
a climax with just his hands and mouth, but she had really
enjoyed those times when he would embed himself within

her. Thrust in and out of her as if he had every right to do so, like her body belonged to him and him alone.

And in a way it had. That was probably why over the past three years, at some of the oddest times, especially late at night when she couldn't sleep, thoughts of him would inflame her mind, her body and her soul. She would ache with an unquenchable longing. She would whisper his name in want, in need, in desire.

Even now, she hadn't made love to another man since Canyon because she hadn't desired another man…not even a little. That had to be why her body was bubbling over with all these crazy hormones now. Why the desire to mate, to have Canyon buried deep inside of her, was so poignant—to the point that it was becoming an emotional thing. And she had promised never to do the emotional thing with any man ever again.

Especially not this man.

Canyon broke eye contact with her, and she followed the direction of his gaze to see a car pulling up the long-winding driveway. She glanced down at her watch. Noon. She moved away from the window. Detective Render had arrived.

After the introductions, Canyon plopped down into one of the living room chairs. Keisha sat on the sofa with her hands clenched together in her lap, and Render sat across from her in another chair. Instead of a notepad, he had opted to use a recorder with Keisha's permission. The man, who appeared to be in his late forties, seemed all business. He was talking into the recorder, giving the date, his location and the reason the interview was about to take place.

Under normal circumstances, one of the police department's sharpest detectives wouldn't waste his time following up on a blatant case of harassment. Not when there were murders to solve. But with Sheriff Harper being such a close friend of Dillon's, and Pete being best friends with Derringer, and Render and Rico sharing a close working relationship, it seemed priority had been given to the incident.

Canyon shifted his gaze from Render to Keisha. As if she'd known the exact moment when he'd done so, she looked over at him. Their gazes held for a long moment and a bond neither of them could deny flowed between them.

At that moment they both knew there was a deeper connection between them than there had been before. It was the result of the little boy sleeping in the bed upstairs. Before, they'd only been lovers. Now they were parents and that was a link neither could break, even if they wanted to.

"Now, Ms. Ashford, let's begin," Detective Render said, causing Keisha to break eye contact with Canyon.

"First of all," Render said, looking at her, "I want to share what I hope is some breaking news. The car that was following you that day as well as the driver of the car have been located. He has been questioned thoroughly."

"Who is he?" It was Canyon who asked before Keisha had a chance to.

Render glanced over at Canyon. "A guy by the name of Shamir Ingram. He has a rap sheet a mile long. We found the car first, with the help of the traffic videos we pulled. And then when an officer recognized the car during a regular patrol, he pulled it over. Ingram was still driving it around with the stolen plate."

"Why did he do it?" Canyon asked.

"Is he the same person who trashed my house?"

Render chuckled when he looked from Canyon to Keisha and then back over to Canyon. "It might be a good idea, Westmoreland, if you joined Ms. Ashford on the sofa so I don't get a whiplash."

"No problem," Canyon said, standing and moving to the sofa. He could have put space between them but decided to sit right beside her. Once he was settled in his seat, Render continued.

"Ingram claims he was paid to follow Ms. Ashford."

"By whom?" Canyon asked, feeling anger toward Ingram invade his body.

"He won't say," Render answered.

"Gone brain-dead, has he?"

"Seems that way. But his cell phone has been confiscated and we're obtaining a search warrant for his place so we can go through his belongings."

Render shifted his gaze from Canyon to Keisha. "Ingram claims he was only paid to follow you and nothing more. His instructions were to freak you out by bumping into your car and running you off the road, but he was not told to trash your house. He guesses someone else was paid to do that."

"I don't believe him," Canyon said angrily.

"I do," Render countered. "I was there during his interrogation. I saw the look of surprise in his eyes when he was questioned about Ms. Ashford's house. And he got riled up at the thought that we were trying to pin both things on him."

"Yet he won't tell you who hired him?" Keisha asked.

"No. He claims he never met the person. The hire was made through a third party."

"What's the name of the third party?"

"He won't say," was Render's reply.

Canyon leaned forward. "Give me some time alone with him and I bet he'll talk."

Render chuckled. "Don't be so sure. A few bruises from you would be nothing in comparison to what he'd get if he's labeled a squealer." Render glanced over at Keisha. "That's why I need to ask you some pertinent questions. Someone is trying to scare you and I need to know why and who."

Keisha nodded. "All right."

"At this point we'll start the recorder," Render said, turning it on. When he was satisfied the equipment was working properly he said, "Ms. Ashford, I understand you moved away from Denver three years ago. Why?"

Keisha frowned. "What does that have to do with anything?"

Render met her gaze without blinking. "I plan to cover all bases and leave no stone unturned."

Keisha nodded and then answered, "I decided Denver was not where I wanted to live any longer."

Canyon knew she had skirted around the real reason she'd left and he had a feeling Render knew it, too.

"Yet, you've returned," Render said.

Canyon felt her tense up beside him before she said, "Yes, I returned. I had to leave my last job and my former boss heard about it and called and offered me my job back here."

Canyon snatched his head around and looked at her. "Why did you have to leave your last job?"

"That's my question, Westmoreland," Render said, grinning. "For the record, Ms. Ashford, why did you need to leave your last job?"

As Canyon and Render watched, Keisha licked her lips nervously. "The law firm was forced to close down."

Render arched a brow. "It went bankrupt?"

Keisha shook her head. "No. The Texas Bar and justice department shut it down."

"Why?" both men asked simultaneously.

Canyon then glanced over at Render and said apologetically, "Sorry."

Render smiled and then looked back to Keisha. "Why

did the Texas Bar and justice department shut down the law firm where you worked?"

Keisha sighed. "It was discovered that several attorneys in the firm—all five partners—abused their power by encouraging their clients to agree to foreclosures and then charging those homeowners exorbitant processing fees. It was later found out that the attorneys were defrauding those clients when the attorneys were receiving kickbacks from the banks, who were reselling the homes at a higher price and making a profit."

"Who turned them in?" Render inquired.

"There were speculations, but the person who exposed them was never identified."

"Was anyone indicted?" Render asked.

"Yes. All five were indicted. My former boss heard about the scandal and knew any law firm in Austin…or Texas for that matter…would be reluctant to hire me on after that."

"Why?" Render asked.

"Although I had nothing to do with what happened and was quickly cleared of any involvement, another firm wouldn't want to bring on an attorney connected to lawyers who were convicted of defrauding clients. So, my former boss offered me my job back."

Canyon said nothing. He'd wondered why she had returned. He knew it hadn't been because she felt Beau needed to be close to his father.

"How long ago did all this happen?" Render asked.

"Ten months ago." Keisha paused. Tilting her head, she stared at Render. "Surely you're not thinking there's a connection between that and what's going on with me now."

With an unreadable expression on his face, Render asked, "Any reason I shouldn't?"

"Of course there is. In fact, there are several," she said, leaning toward him.

Holding her gaze, Render said, "Name them."

Keisha pulled back and nodded. "Okay. First of all, those fraudulent activities were going on before I was even hired there and I never worked any of the cases. I was one of three relatively new attorneys. Second, those who were indicted were all partners. The other two attorneys, like me, were freshmen attorneys, considered to be peons. We were clueless as to what the top brass was doing. Third, why would anyone connected with that incident want to scare me? Scare me away from what? Why me? And who would be orchestrating such a thing?"

Render smiled. "First of all, I never said I had made a connection. You're the one who offered reasons why there is no connection, and I just asked you to name them. My job is to gather the facts, Ms. Ashford. All of them. And I agree that the chances of what happened yesterday being connected to what happened with that law firm in Texas is farfetched. But like I told you, I'm leaving no stone unturned." He paused. "But before you completely discount the possibility of a connection, let me give you this to consider. The attorneys were indicted, but I assume they haven't gone to trial?"

Keisha lifted a brow. "How would you know that?"

He chuckled. "We're talking about attorneys." Then, as if he remembered both Canyon and Keisha were attorneys, he smiled and said, "No offense, but I'm convinced these particular attorneys would use their knowledge of the law to delay serving time for as long as they can. They would also use their knowledge of the law to build a defense…while they're putting the fear of God in the whistle-blower."

Puzzlement appeared on her features. "But I wasn't the whistle-blower."

Render smiled. "Would they know that? Which makes me wonder if the other two freshmen attorneys not involved in the crimes have experienced scare tactics, too? Do the three of you keep in touch?"

She shook her head. "No. I never developed any close relationships with them. They were single and partiers and I was a mother with a newborn at home."

"Give me their names. It would be worth checking to see if they're being harassed, as well."

She gave him the man's and woman's names. Render then leaned back in his chair. "And just in case that's a theory leading nowhere, let's talk about the cases you've handled since returning to Denver?"

Keisha's eyes widened. "All of them?"

"As many as you can remember that might have resulted in ill feelings with clients or plaintiffs."

Three hours later, Ervin Render stood and stretched his body. "Well, I think I have a lot of information to go on."

Keisha frowned. She thought he had more than enough. He had picked her brain dry while almost making her suspect that any of her clients could be the culprit. Beau had wakened a couple of hours ago and she now glanced over to where he was on the floor staring at all the species of fish in the huge tank.

"If I have any more questions, I'll reach you here," Render added.

"You can try my mobile number because I won't be here," she said, standing as well when Canyon came to stand beside her.

Render lifted a brow. "Where will you be?"

"Probably at a hotel until I get my house back in order. Is there a problem?"

He shrugged and glanced from her to Canyon and back again. "Not for me, but it might be for you."

"In what way?" It was Canyon who spoke up with the question.

Render shoved his hands into his pockets. "We still don't know who hired Ingram to scare Ms. Ashford or who was responsible for trashing her house. If I were her, I wouldn't go anywhere alone."

That was not what Keisha wanted to hear. Nor was that what she wanted Canyon to hear. "I have a life, Detective Render," she said. "I can't give in to scare tactics."

"No, and you shouldn't," the man said easily. "But then you shouldn't make yourself a target either, Ms. Ashford. Until we know who's behind this, you should stay low for a while."

"That's not possible," she said, lifting her chin. "I work and have a job to do."

Render didn't say anything. Instead he glanced at Beau and then moved his gaze back to her. "You also have a son to raise, and I'm sure you want to be around to do so. I suggest you take a week off from work and don't go anywhere by yourself."

Keisha slowly drew in a breath. "Surely you're not suggesting that someone would—"

"I'm not suggesting anything. I'm just letting you know the possibilities. Someone wanted to scare you off. The reason why is still a mystery. Until you know what or who you're dealing with, you should hang around people you know, ones who have your back. Think about it. No need to bother showing me out. I know my way."

Canyon walked the man to the door anyway, while a frustrated Keisha worked the kinks out of her neck. She had to go to a hotel. There was no way she could stay under Canyon's roof another night.

She glanced up when he reentered the room. She opened her mouth to tell him she was going to a hotel in spite of what Render had said when he stopped her.

"I heard what Render said, Keisha, and there's nothing to think about. You're staying."

He then turned and walked out of the room.

An angry Keisha followed Canyon to the kitchen but hung back to stand in the doorway so she could also keep an eye on Beau, who was still lying on the living room floor staring at the huge fish tank.

"You don't tell me what to do," she said in a near whisper. "And I'm leaving."

Canyon walked back to her. "No, you're not. Did you not hear what Render said? Why are you being so damn stubborn?" he asked in a low, infuriated tone.

She lifted her chin. "I am not being stubborn, just practical. I can't stay here."

"Can you give me one good reason why you can't?"

There was no way she would tell him the real reason, mainly that being around him did crazy things to her hormones and made her remember feelings she just couldn't shake.

"Well?"

She frowned. He was standing there with his arms over his chest, facing her down like she was an unruly child. "For all I know, you might be involved with someone who might resent my being here."

He stared at her as if she'd lost her mind and then he said, "I'm not involved with anyone, and even if I was, do you think I'd let that person sway me to put my son's life in danger? Or to put the mother of my child in danger?"

Keisha swallowed. In a way, it hurt that all she was to him now was the mother of his child. There once was a time when she had been more. But that was before he'd allowed another woman to come between them.

"I can't stay here, Canyon. And you can't force me to stay. Nor can you threaten to take Beau from me if I leave with him."

Instead of addressing anything she'd said, he informed her in a low tone, "You still haven't given me a good reason why you can't stay here, Keisha. I told you I wasn't involved with anyone. I live in this big house by myself. I'll have my side and you'll have yours. What are you afraid of?"

She bristled at his question. "I'm not afraid of anything."

He ran a frustrated hand over his face and sighed. "Then think sensibly for a moment. Sure you can go to a hotel, but Beau will have more space here. He has family here. Why are you so determined to keep him away from me? Do you hate me that much?"

Something twisted inside of her. There wasn't a grain of truth in his assumption, and there was no way she could allow him to think that there was. "No. I don't hate you at all, Canyon. I admit when I left here I was angry and hurt. I felt betrayed. And I kept feeling that way with all those emotions festering inside of me. Then one day something happened," she said softly.

He lifted a brow. "What?"

She drew in a deep breath. "I felt my baby move. The baby you had put inside of me. I realized it was a real life, and I knew I couldn't feel so angry with you anymore because, at that moment, regardless of how things ended between us, you'd given me something you could never take away."

Canyon dropped his arms. "Is that why you don't want

to include me in your and Beau's world…because you think I'd take him away from you?"

She took a long, shuddering breath before narrowing her gaze at him. "You said as much just last night."

"We said a lot of things last night, Keisha. I'm sure today there are regrets on both our parts. I don't want to take Beau from you. I want to share him with you. But first I want to keep you both safe. Please let me do that. Stay here for at least a week to see how things work out. Hopefully by then Detective Render's investigation will provide more answers. Then, who knows, it might be safe for you to go home."

"And if it's not?"

"We will reevaluate your options then."

Keisha knew she shouldn't consider his offer. There was no way she could remain a week under his roof without fear of losing her sanity. But would it be fair to place Beau in danger just because she couldn't keep her hormones in check?

She switched her gaze from Canyon's intense features to Beau. He had finally grown tired of lying on his stomach staring at the fish tank and was now on his back playing with the toy Denver—by way of Denver's parents—had loaned Beau.

She loved her child more than life, and she had to keep him safe until she knew what she was up against. And there was only one way to do that.

Canyon.

She might not be his favorite person right now, but he would do anything to protect his son.

She looked back at Canyon and met his dark, penetrating gaze. "All right," she said softly. "Beau and I will stay for a week."

Eight

Keisha eased out of bed. No matter how tired she was, she just couldn't seem to fall asleep and now she had one of those headaches she often got when she was stressed about something. All she could think about was how Detective Render had cast suspicions that now stirred in her mind, from her last job to every case she'd worked since returning to Denver.

What if one of the attorney's at that law firm in Texas had actually thought she was the whistle-blower and was trying to get back at her? Or what if the harassment had something to do with the case she'd won last year when she'd proved her client was the owner of land that a huge car dealership sat on?

Her client hadn't accepted the dealership owner's offer to lease the property. Instead her client had wanted the property vacated immediately, which could have caused hardship to the owner of the dealership. Bryant Knowles hadn't been happy with her and had accused her of intentionally advising her client not to negotiate with opposing counsel. That hadn't been true, but nothing she said could convince Knowles otherwise. The two finally reached an agreement that was satisfactory to both in the end, but what if Knowles still harbored ill feelings?

Keisha glanced over at Beau. At least one of them had no problem sleeping tonight.

After she'd made her decision about staying, Canyon had gone to the store to purchase a safety gate for the stairs as well as cabinet locks, corner protectors, electrical outlet covers and a number of other items. While he was doing that, she had placed a call to Pam, letting her know she would need to go shopping tomorrow after all since she and Beau would be down to their last outfits.

When Canyon returned, he immediately went to work childproofing his house. And he'd purchased toys that had kept Beau entertained for the rest of the day. While he was out, Canyon had picked up carryout from McKays, a popular restaurant in town, which had taken the guesswork out of what they would have for dinner.

Grabbing her robe off a chair, she left the bedroom, securing the safety gate in place before going down the stairs. Except for the night-lights Canyon had installed, the rooms were completely dark, but Keisha had no problem finding her way to the kitchen. Canyon had left the curtains open, which gave her a full view of the moonlit sky.

The first time Canyon had brought her to visit this piece of land it had been at night and except for a few grassy areas the land had been wooded. They had parked and talked under the huge sky dotted with beautiful stars. And later they had made out in the car under that same sky. That night they had initiated their own private lover's lane.

Now Canyon had built a home here, possibly on the

same spot because it sure as heck looked like the same sky. She knew that sounded crazy, but she was convinced this portion of sky belonged only to Canyon's Bluff.

"Couldn't sleep either?"

Keisha swung around when Canyon walked into the kitchen. She was immediately slammed with an overabundance of lust when she saw what he was…not wearing. He was in his bare feet, shirtless with his drawstring pajama bottoms riding low on his hips and clinging to a pair of powerful thighs.

The moonlight coming through the window encased him in a sensuous glow. Tingling sensations bombarded the area between her legs. Heated lust flared through her bloodstream and instinctively she pressed her thighs together.

Drawing in a shaky breath, she said, "No, having one of those headaches."

"Oh."

He knew about her headaches since she'd had them in the past when things hadn't gone quite like she'd wanted at work and she'd gotten stressed out about it.

"Come and sit down," he said, pulling out a chair from the table.

She glanced at the chair and then back at him. She knew what he wanted to do. Whenever she'd had a headache, Canyon used to rub her temples and ease the nagging pain away. She didn't know how he did it, but he would do it every time.

"Keisha?"

She swallowed. At the moment, headache or no headache, the last thing she could handle was Canyon's hands on her. But even as she had that thought, a fierce, agonizing throb pierced through her head, propelling her to move toward the chair. As soon as she sat down, she inhaled his masculine scent and instinctively breathed in deeper to pull in the heady aroma.

"Now close your eyes and relax," he said in a low, throaty tone that sent a ripple through her. She released a low groan when she felt his fingers slowly rake through her hair. She closed her eyes when she felt the heat of him behind her, gently massaging her scalp and placing light pressure at her temples. He kept up the kneading, working out the pain and soothing the ache.

He leaned down. "Feeling better?" he asked in an incredibly sexy voice, while the warmth of his breath fanned the side of her face.

Unable to respond, she nodded. The gentle scalp massage sent delicious shivers through her, replacing one kind of ache with another. She recalled the last time he'd done this. It had been a little more than three years ago. She had been stuck in litigation with what she thought was the case from hell. The opposing counsel had tried more than once to belittle her in front of the jury and she'd fought to retain her cool, which had resulted in an overpowering headache.

When she'd gotten home, Canyon had sat her down at the kitchen table and massaged her scalp and temples. By the time it was over, he had gotten rid of her headache but had left her wanting him…like he was doing now. Back then, he'd pulled her out of the chair, stripped her naked, laid her out on the table and made mind-blowing love to her.

"You can open your eyes now. And if you follow this up with an aspirin, you'll feel good as new in the morning."

Drawing in a shaky breath she slowly opened her eyes. *What about tonight?* Would she feel as good as new tonight, too? She didn't think so…not as long as the tingling between her legs continued.

"Thanks, Canyon."

"You're welcome."

Keisha eased up from her chair and he slid it back under the table. She turned toward him. "You have a special touch," she said and then wished she could bite off her tongue for saying so.

His lips slowly spread into a smile, revealing a dimple that was normally kept hidden. "You think so?"

There was that sexy voice again that made her shiver. "Yes."

He chuckled softly. "Glad you still approve…of my hands…and what they are capable of doing."

She swallowed, wishing he hadn't gone there. "Well, I guess I'll go back upstairs."

"All right."

Why was she still standing there? Keisha asked herself. Why couldn't her feet move? Why was Canyon pinning her with those gorgeous dark eyes? And why was she standing there staring back?

She didn't remember who made the first move, all she knew was that it was made. He slid his warm arms around her, drawing her to him. And knowing what was coming next, her lips twitched, eager to be joined with his. He lowered his head and the connection was made with a precision that sent shivers all through her. She wrapped her arms around his neck as his tongue eased between her lips.

She groaned when he deepened the kiss as hunger sent blood rushing through her veins. She'd known after their first kiss that no man kissed like Canyon. This was his calling, and she was a willing recipient. Her mind was flooded with memories…but this kiss was even better.

Keisha forgot about her vow to never let Canyon Westmoreland get close to her again. To never let him hold her, kiss her or make her moan. Because, at that moment, he was doing all three. And she was powerless to resist.

He deepened the kiss and heat flowed from his body to hers, setting the lower part of her body on fire. She felt his strong thighs pressing against her and thought, *Lordy*. His thick, hard shaft was cradled between her thighs, feeling as if it belonged there. Right there. Only Canyon had the power to manipulate her desires to his will and play havoc with her emotions.

And then suddenly, he broke off the kiss and his hands fell from her waist. The disconnect was so sudden she almost lost her balance. He quickly reached out to keep her from falling and she gasped when it hit her full force what they'd done. What she had let him do. She had to get away from him, to put distance between them, and she needed to do it now.

"I'm going back to bed," she said, backing up slowly. "Thanks for the head rub." She turned and was almost out of the kitchen when his words stopped her.

"Trust me, Keisha."

She stopped walking, tightening the robe around her and turning around. "What?"

"If the reason you got that headache is because you're worried about all the suspicions Detective Render raised, then I want you to believe that I won't let anyone hurt you or Beau. I want you to trust me about that."

Trust him? She drew in a trembling breath. The same man who'd betrayed her with another woman wanted her to trust him? A frown lined her brow, but as she stared at him, she saw something in the depth of his dark eyes that made the frown dissolve.

He wouldn't let anyone hurt her or Beau. She could trust him regarding that.

Without saying anything, she nodded before turning and quickly walking out of the kitchen.

* * *

Canyon watched Keisha leave while licking his lips, savoring the taste she had left behind. She'd left her fragrance behind as well, and it was just as arousing. It didn't help matters that when she'd tightened the robe, she'd emphasized her full breasts, her trim waist and her curvy hips. And then when she'd walked out of the kitchen the material had stretched across one delectable-looking backside.

His memory had been jogged, remembering scenes of that same body in several other outfits…like that short, slinky red dress she'd worn when he'd accompanied her to her firm's Christmas party several years back, and that short, black lace dress she'd worn to the Westmoreland Ball.

And then there was a flash from the past of that body wearing nothing at all. Now, *that* was a memory that had his body getting hard, making him want things he was better off not having. Especially when those things concerned Keisha. There was no place for this fierce hunger or for the assault on his senses that had come from kissing her.

But he could no more not kiss her than he could stop his heart from beating. Touching her, running his fingers through her hair, listening to her moan had pushed him over the edge, had made hot, potent lust flare up within him. Desire had taken control of his brain. Yes, kissing her had been foolish, but it had also been a detriment to his peace of mind. If he'd thought he couldn't sleep before, he sure as hell wouldn't be able to sleep now.

Moving across the kitchen, he went to the refrigerator and pulled out a beer and popped the tab. Hell, he truly needed something stronger but he would settle for this. It had been one hell of a day and was moving into one hell of a night. He'd missed most of it already.

He glanced over at the clock on the stove and saw it was

just about midnight. He'd thought it was later than that. But who could keep time when it was taking all his effort to keep a level head around Keisha. He'd known Detective Render's visit had left her pretty uptight. Hell, who wouldn't be uptight, considering someone had paid a pair of goons to send her into a panic.

Before going to the store, Canyon had made a pit stop at Dillon's to tell him about Detective Render's visit and what had transpired. Dillon agreed that keeping Keisha and Beau within arm's reach here in Westmoreland Country was the best thing. He figured it would be advantageous if the Westmoreland men met to come up with a plan. Dillon had made the calls and within half an hour his brothers and cousins had arrived. They'd decided that if Canyon couldn't be with Keisha, one of the other Westmoreland men would be.

Now, tilting the can of beer to his lips, Canyon took a long, pleasurable gulp, licked his lips and frowned. Why could he still taste Keisha? Hell. Would he ever find peace from the woman? Evidently not, and now she was under his roof and would be for another week. And it had been his choice. He had asked, and she had reluctantly agreed. Now she was here and he had to decide how he felt about it.

If tonight was anything to go by, then what he was feeling were emotions that he shouldn't be feeling. This was a woman who thought he had betrayed her, a woman who hadn't told him he had a son even when she'd had every opportunity to do so.

Yet at the same time, he thought, taking another gulp of beer, Keisha Ashford was a woman he would protect with his life if he had to. It would be easier to protect her if she was here…and if he could keep himself from kissing her again.

Nine

"So, what do you think of this outfit, Keisha?"

Keisha glanced over at the clothes. Lucia held up a pair of little boy's jeans with a miniature work shirt to match. It was cute, and she could see Beau wearing it. She smiled. "I like it. Do they have it in a 3T?" Although Beau was two, because of his height he was wearing a size larger.

"Yes, I'll grab one for you," Lucia said excitedly.

Keisha grinned as she watched Lucia. Keisha obviously wasn't the only woman who liked shopping for her child. She was convinced the Westmoreland ladies had her beat. They had shown up on Canyon's doorstep at one o'clock with Canyon's younger brother Stern following behind them. Stern was only twenty months younger than Canyon and also an attorney at their family-owned firm, Blue Ridge.

Stern had advised the women that he was their escort for the day, and since none of them had questioned what he'd meant by that, Keisha could only assume everyone had been told of Detective Render's visit and his warning. Until they found out who was responsible for the craziness going on with her, it would be best if she took every precaution when it came to her and Beau's safety. And she was discovering the Westmorelands believed in looking after their own. The idea that she was now included in the mix because she was Beau's mother was mind-boggling.

So now she was in Kiddies' World Boutique surrounded by five women, who if Keisha wasn't careful could become her new BFFs. She'd taken a chance on Bonita after they'd met at a spa when she'd moved to Denver the first time and look what had happened. It had taken her a long time to even consider making new friends again.

"Think we got enough things for Beau?" Pam asked, coming up to Keisha holding outfits she'd grabbed off the racks for her sons Denver and Dade.

Keisha couldn't help but grin. "We bought too much if you ask me."

"Well, you heard Canyon's orders to get whatever you wanted," Chloe said, tossing the outfit for Beau in Keisha's cart and a cute little dress for her daughter, Susan, in hers.

Yes, he had said that, but it hadn't made her happy. She couldn't help frowning at the memory. When Canyon had offered her his charge card, she had refused to take it, telling him that she could pay for Beau's things without his help. He'd merely slid the card into her shirt pocket and said, "Humor me," before walking off.

"For what it's worth, I agree you should humor him, like he said, Keisha," Pam said softly. "He wants to feel he's doing something for Beau."

Keisha released a sigh. "He did something for Beau yesterday. You should see all the stuff he brought back from the store. He got plenty of safety items, but he also bought Beau a lot of toys he didn't need."

"Sure Beau will need them," a pregnant Kalina said, grinning. "Kids can't have too many toys."

"It's the grown men you have to worry about," Bella said, smiling. "Jason asked his cousin Thorn to build him a motorcycle."

"Um, you ladies ought to check out Micah's speedboat back in D.C.," Kalina said, laughing.

Keisha was amused when each woman told a story about their husband's favorite new toy. She saw how easy it was for them to laugh at themselves and with each other, and she knew this was what she'd missed out on by not belonging to a big family—a special connection, a cama-raderie and a closeness that extended to the women who had married into it.

She glanced to where Stern was sitting in a chair near the entrance of the shop, his legs stretched out in front of him and his Stetson riding low on his head while he talked on his cell phone. Like his brothers and cousins, Stern was tall and ultra-handsome. He had long lashes to die for and a smile that could snatch a woman's breath right out of her lungs.

He didn't seem the least perturbed at having to hang out with a bunch of women today. And he hadn't gotten in the way. This was the second store they'd visited and at both locations he'd hung back, grabbed a chair and sat near the entrance while talking on the phone. But she was fully aware of his alert gaze, which had checked out all the people moving in and out of the store. His actions reminded her of just how serious her predicament was. It might be a while before the police found out who'd targeted her, and she couldn't expect a member of the Westmoreland family to be her bodyguard that whole time.

"Keisha?"

She shifted her gaze back to the women and found them staring at her. "Yes?"

"We're not trying to get in your business, because heaven knows all of us have had our ups and downs with Westmoreland men. But is there a reason you didn't want Canyon to know about Beau? We know about that incident you walked in on with that woman. We're not judging. But still, didn't you think he had a right to know about Beau?" Pam asked softly.

Keisha tried not to be defensive. She bit back the impulse to tell them to mind their own business. These women had befriended her when they didn't have to. They had been nothing but kind to her. Even Bailey, who'd joined them at the first shop they'd visited before leaving to meet a friend for lunch, had been nicer to her today.

All of the women before her had married Westmoreland men. Megan, the only married Westmoreland sister who still lived in Denver, hadn't been able to join them because she'd been called to the hospital this morning as the anesthesiologist for an emergency surgery.

Keisha wondered how she could explain her reasons so that they would understand. "When I left Denver three years ago, I was hurt and felt betrayed. I didn't want to see Canyon ever again, and I wanted no contact with him. I was determined to have my child without any man's help, like my mother did. I thought at the time that Canyon didn't deserve anything from me. As far as I was concerned, he'd lost any rights to his child." She paused. "I now admit that I was wrong to feel that way."

Admitting she was wrong about something she'd believed so strongly at the time was a big move for her. "If I had to do it again I would handle things differently. No matter how or why our relationship ended, I should have told Canyon about Beau."

There, she'd said it. All it had taken was to see Canyon's interactions with his son over the past forty-eight hours to know how good they were for each other. Beau's acceptance of Canyon had been quick and absolute, and the same thing could be said of Canyon's acceptance of Beau.

Pam gently touched Keisha's shoulder. "That's a start, Keisha."

Was it? Keisha asked herself more than once over the next four hours they spent shopping.

There was still the issue of Canyon's betrayal. She had forced that nightmare out of her mind and had refused to consider that she'd been wrong. But what had she really seen? Although she hadn't caught Canyon and Bonita in bed together, Bonita had been naked, and Canyon had walked out of the bathroom with a towel around his middle.

Hadn't that been enough? Why would Bonita lie and say she and Canyon had slept together when they hadn't?

"You okay, Keisha?" Pam asked with concern in her voice as they made a turn onto the road leading to Canyon's Bluff.

"Yes, I'm okay," Keisha replied, but she wasn't. She felt a headache coming on, similar to the one she'd had last night. The same one Canyon had relieved her of...before he'd kissed her.

She took her tongue and licked her top lip, still feeling the aftertaste of pleasure. After she'd gone back to bed, the ache in her head was gone but the ache between her legs had been almost unbearable. It had been an hour later before she'd finally drifted off to sleep with dreams of endless sex with Canyon flowing through her mind.

"We're here. Looks like your guys are waiting on you."

Keisha glanced out the car window and felt a flutter in her stomach when she saw father and son sitting side by side on the porch, leaning back on their arms with their legs swinging simultaneously while watching the car pull up. Both had similar huge smiles on their faces. She understood why Beau was smiling. He was glad to see her. But why was Canyon smiling?

She couldn't imagine that he was glad to see her. She knew he'd been kind enough to provide shelter to her and Beau for the next week, but she knew the only reason he had was because he wanted to protect his son. She just happened to be part of the package.

As soon as she opened the car door, Beau charged across the yard to her. "Mommy! Mommy! You home, Mommy!"

She raised a brow. *Home?* Beau had only been here for two days and he already thought of Canyon's place as home. What about her house? Granted the last time he'd seen it, it had been a mess, but still…

"Yes, Mommy is here," she said, smiling down at him. "Were you a good boy?"

"Yes, good boy. Daddy-Dad has horse. Big horse," he said, widening his arms. "I ride."

Keisha chuckled. "Did you?"

"Yes." He turned toward Canyon. "Didn't I, Daddy-Dad?"

"You most certainly did."

Keisha watched as Canyon eased off the porch, and she felt a tingling in the pit of her stomach when his jeans stretched tight across his muscled thighs. She couldn't ignore the rush of desire that poured through her as she stared at him walking toward her with a stride so sexy she felt flushed by its heat.

"Well, we'll be going now," Pam said, reclaiming Keisha's attention.

She glanced at Pam and all the other women staring at her with a "we understand" smile on their faces. "Okay, and thank you all for everything."

"No problem. Jill is leaving early tomorrow morning, and she and I plan to do a movie tonight. At least I don't have to get up and take her to the airport. Aiden is such a sweetie. He volunteered to take Jill for me," Pam said, getting back behind the wheel of the van.

"I bet he did," Keisha heard Canyon mutter under his breath as Pam drove off. She glanced at him, wondering what he meant by that. He had come to stand beside her. He looked good, and he smelled good. It was a powerful combination.

Keisha then looked at Stern who'd gotten out of his car to help the ladies remove the shopping bags. "Thank you, Stern."

He gave her a sexy smile. "My pleasure."

"Looks like you bought a lot," Canyon said in a throaty voice, moving past her to take the shopping bags from Stern.

"I took your advice and decided to humor you."

Canyon threw his head back and laughed. "Thanks."

"Well, I hate to run, but I'm meeting JoJo in town. We're attending that Muscle Car Show," Stern said, opening the door to his car and sliding inside.

"Thanks, Stern," Canyon said.

"No problem. Lucky for all of you that I didn't have a date or anything," Stern said, grinning. Giving them a wave, he then drove off.

Keisha glanced over at Canyon. "Who's JoJo?"

"His best friend, Jovonnie Jones. They have been friends since they were kids in middle school. Her father owned an auto mechanic shop in town, but she took things over when Mr. Jones passed away."

Keisha lifted her brow. "She's a mechanic?"

"The best. She works on all our cars," he said, turning toward the house. "Where do you want these?"

"Up in my bedroom. I mean the bedroom you're letting me use," she corrected.

"I knew what you meant, Keisha. Did you buy something for yourself, as well?"

"Yes, but I didn't put it on your charge card. I used my own, but thanks for the offer." She glanced down at Beau, whose hand she was holding firmly in hers as they went up the steps to the porch. She looked back at Canyon. "Was Beau a good boy?"

"Of course. All Westmorelands are good," he said, grinning.

She rolled her eyes. "So you say."

"So I know. And speaking of Westmorelands, there's something I want to discuss with you," he said, opening the door and gesturing for her to go in front of him.

She released Beau's hand when he tugged for her to let go. She watched him scamper off to the living room where he flipped down on his stomach to stare at the huge fish tank, which was becoming his favorite pastime. Canyon had purchased several fish to add to the tank yesterday and that had fascinated Beau even more.

When Canyon returned from placing the bags upstairs, he found her sitting down at the dining room table. "So what do you want to talk with me about, Canyon?" she asked, wondering what his discussion would involve.

Instead of sitting down across from her, he shoved his hands into the pockets of his jeans and leaned back against the huge breakfast bar that separated the dining room from the kitchen.

"It's about Beau."

Her stomach knotted at the serious look in his eyes and the firm set of his jaw. "What about Beau?"

"I want my son to have my name, Keisha."

She swallowed. "Your name?"

"Yes. He's a Westmoreland, and I want his last name to reflect that."

Canyon knew he had a fight on his hands, but he was ready for the battle. He had thought about it from day one and felt justified in what he was asking. There was no reason for his son not to have his name.

He waited and watched Keisha study the floor before looking back up at him. "All right."

He blinked, surprised at her response. "All right?"

"Yes, all right." She stood. "I'm sure Beau hasn't had a nap yet so I'll take him up—"

"Whoa. Wait a minute," he said, straightening away from the breakfast bar.

"Yes?"

"Why?" he asked.

She lifted a brow. "Why what?"

He gave her a level look. "Why are you being so charitable all of a sudden?"

She stiffened her spine. "Did you think I wouldn't agree to it?"

"Yes."

She held his stare and then turned away for a second before turning back to find his gaze searching her face. "Well?" he asked, staring her down.

She eased down into her chair. "I owe you an apology, Canyon."

More surprise flashed in his eyes. "Do you?"

"Yes. Beau is your son and no matter how things ended between us, I should have told you about him."

Canyon froze. Of all the things he had expected her to say, that wasn't it. She was right. She should have told him about Beau. "Is that the only thing you're apologizing for?"

He watched her lift her chin. She fully understood what he was asking. Was she also apologizing for believing he had betrayed her?

"Yes, that's the only thing I'm apologizing for."

He stared at her for a long moment. In other words, she still believed him to be a cheating bastard. One day she would realize just how wrong she was about him. When that day came, what would she do? Would she think any words of apology could erase what she had put him through? Had put them both through?

Holding in the anger he was feeling, he said, "I'll contact a man who handles all the Westmorelands' legal affairs. He will complete the paperwork for the change."

"That's fine."

He bit back the words to tell her that she was wrong. It wasn't fine. At that moment, he wasn't sure if things between them could ever be fine again.

"Honest, Mom. Beau and I are okay," Keisha said, talking into her cell phone. She and her mother made a point of talking every Sunday afternoon and Keisha knew she should tell Lynn what was going on.

"And the police have no idea who's responsible?" Lynn asked.

"Not yet, but they're on top of this."

"So you and Beau are living at a hotel?"

Keisha nibbled on her bottom lip. "No, we aren't at a hotel."

"Then where are you?"

Releasing a deep sigh, Keisha spent the next fifteen minutes telling her mother everything, including her recent apology to Canyon for not telling him about Beau.

When she finished, Lynn didn't say anything for a long moment. "I'm glad everything's out now, Keisha. I never felt you should keep Beau a secret from his father."

"I know, Mom, but during that time the pain was more than I could bear."

"I know, baby, but he had that right. Even I knew better than to do that to your father."

"Yes, but what good did it do?" Keisha asked curtly. "How could he have believed I wasn't his?" It was something she had wondered about, but had never asked.

"Because I was supposed to be on birth control, and he didn't want to believe it hadn't worked. And, unfortunately, at the time a woman had accused his older brother of the same thing and they'd found out she was lying."

"But he loved you, so he should have believed you," Keisha said fiercely.

"Um, that's easy for you to say. You loved Canyon, yet you didn't believe him when he denied sleeping with that woman."

Her mother's words were a blow that Keisha felt in her belly, nearly knocking the wind out of her. "My situation was different," she defended softly, while her insides struggled for normalcy.

"Was it?"

"Yes." Keisha glanced out the kitchen window, again wondering if she'd done the right thing by staying here and not at a hotel. It was getting dark, but Canyon was still outside. She could see him working in his yard. Earlier, he had washed down the barn with a hose and before that he had washed his car. He was working off his anger. She understood and accepted his actions.

"I don't see how. You never saw them in bed together and only went with what that woman said. Getting back to your father, when he saw you for the first time, he knew you were his."

"Yes, but I was fifteen by then." She had gone over this with her mother plenty of times. Granted, her mother had moved away from Texas, which had made it impossible for her father to see her, but as far as she was concerned the timing and the distance had been his fault. All he'd had to do that day when they'd run into him and his brother in a restaurant was to look at her to know how wrong he'd been. He had spent the past fourteen years since that day trying to undo that wrong. But she'd refused to meet him halfway. A part of her couldn't let go of how he'd rejected her before she'd been born.

Needing to change the subject, she asked her mother how things were going at the hospital where she'd worked for more than twenty years. Keisha then inquired about the ladies who'd worked with her for years and whom Keisha considered honorary aunties. The same women who'd been there to give their support during Lynn's breast cancer scare. She knew her mother wanted to return to their discussion of both Canyon and her father, but Lynn knew when to back off. After all, Keisha was her mother's daughter, and although the mother might have mellowed over the years, her daughter had not.

When Keisha heard the kitchen door open and close she didn't have to turn around to know Canyon had come inside. "Okay, Mom, we'll talk again later. It's time for me to put Beau to bed."

"All right, sweetheart. Tell Beau that Gramma loves him. And say hello to Canyon for me."

Keisha nodded. "I will."

Keisha clicked off her phone and slowly swiveled

around. Canyon was leaning against the refrigerator with his hands shoved in the pockets of his jeans, staring at her. A rush of awareness swept through her. It sizzled her insides and sent a gush of blood through her veins. "That was Mom. She told me to tell you hello."

He nodded and said nothing.

"Beau wanted to wait until you came in to eat."

Canyon glanced around. "Where is he?"

"Sitting at the dining room table listening to his books." Canyon had bought Beau a stack of audio storybooks with colorful pictures, which he was enjoying. "I'll let him know you're here so he can eat and get into bed at a reasonable time."

She made a move to walk past Canyon and he snagged her arm. When she glanced up at him, he moved to stand directly in front of her.

"I accept your apology."

Ten

Keisha was still mulling over Canyon's words hours later, even after she'd taken a shower and gotten into bed. Why did his acceptance of her apology make her feel worse instead of better? And why did her mother have to bring up her father?

A mental image of the man who'd fathered her flashed through Keisha's mind. The physical resemblance was there for even a half-blind man to see. She had her father's eyes, nose, lips and forehead. He'd seen it that day, and she had seen it for herself. That day he had discovered just what a fool he'd been to think her mother had betrayed him. The sad thing was that it had taken him fifteen years to realize the truth.

Since then, he'd made several attempts to reach out to her, but she didn't want anything to do with him. She'd even gotten upset when she'd found out her mother had given in and let him back into her life. Her mother didn't think Keisha knew, but she did.

Easing out of bed, Keisha decided to go downstairs and grab her ereader off the coffee table where she'd left it earlier. It was past midnight, so she would read a novel until she got sleepy. She didn't have any court cases this week, which was good, and she had spoken to Mr. Whitock. After explaining the situation, he had agreed that she should take the week off.

Sliding into her robe, she checked on Beau one last time before leaving the room to go downstairs.

Canyon stood at his bedroom window, staring up at the sky. He resented the seesaw of emotions coursing through him. One minute he was filled with so much anger about all Keisha had done, and then the next minute he was overcome by a need for her that could erupt into desire with very little effort.

And that kiss last night hadn't helped matters. It had only proved that the physical chemistry between them was stronger than ever. His need had flared up so swiftly he could have taken her then and there. That was why he had ended the kiss the way he had. His desire for her had been so sharp it had cut into everything, including his common sense. She could ignite desire in him without even trying.

Like earlier that day, when he'd come in from outside and she'd been talking on the phone to her mother. He had stood leaning against the refrigerator, feeling tightness in his loins. A warm rush of heat had flowed through him. She looked damn good in her jeans, which emphasized her lush curves and shapely backside. He could have ogled her for hours. And when she'd turned around he'd been captured by her incredibly beautiful face. His senses had been reduced to mush.

And then he had accepted her apology. While he was working off his anger outside, he had remembered how he and his brothers used to fuss and fight and how his mother would make them apologize to each other. His mother always told them not to apologize or accept an apology if they didn't really mean it.

Canyon rubbed a hand down his face. He had accepted Keisha's apology because he believed she'd been sincere in making it and regretted keeping Beau from him. To continue to feel bitterness and anger toward her wasn't healthy, not for him and not for his son. And very quickly Beau had become the most important person in his life.

As far as the issue of Keisha still believing that he was a cheating bastard, that was something that would not keep him up at night. She could think whatever she wanted, he didn't care anymore. As long as she didn't keep him from his son then he could deal with anything else. Besides, he no longer loved her. But he did want her. Lusty thoughts were keeping him up, making it hard to sleep. He'd already told Dillon he was taking tomorrow off. He had spoken with Roy McDonald, who had agreed to meet with him and Keisha at noon tomorrow to complete the paperwork to change Beau's last name.

When he'd mentioned the appointment to Keisha earlier tonight she'd said she would need Beau's birth certificate, which was at her home. So he would take her there in the morning to get it. He'd gotten the okay from Pete earlier yesterday that all prints had been lifted and it was okay for Keisha to bring order to her home. Canyon had already made arrangements to take care of that, as well.

He stretched his body, deciding to go downstairs and walk outside for a while. Seeing the sky from his bedroom window was nice, but on a night like this he preferred being beneath it.

* * *

Keisha made it across the living room before she collided with a hard muscled body. A spark of desire flashed through her the moment they touched. When she reached out to grab Canyon, to stop herself from falling, she touched his bare chest and heard his quick intake of breath. His arms went around her waist to steady her.

"Oh, sorry, Canyon. I didn't know you were still up."

"I wasn't. I couldn't sleep and thought I would take a stroll outside," he said in a deep, husky voice.

"Oh. And I came downstairs to grab my ereader off the table where I left it earlier."

"Couldn't sleep again?" he asked.

"No, I couldn't sleep again." Why were they still standing here with her hands on his chest and his hands around her waist? And why was his heart beating so fast beneath her palms and why was hers beating just as rapidly? And why were so many too-lusty thoughts flowing through her brain, causing heat to stir and making every cell in her body throb as she inhaled his manly scent?

"You want to go with me outside?" he whispered.

She swallowed. She couldn't. She shouldn't. But in an instant, she knew that she would. Dropping her hands from his chest, she said, "Okay."

He let go of her waist and entwined his hand with hers. "Come on." He led her across the room and out the door.

The moment they stepped onto the porch Canyon stopped to breathe in the warm August night air. He then glanced up at the sky and a sense of calm flowed through him. Something else flowed through him, as well. An affirmation of the thoughts he'd had earlier this evening.

"This sky still holds special meaning to you, doesn't it?"

He glanced over at her. "You remember?"

She chuckled softly. "How could I not. Because of you, I've grown fond of the sky, as well. I haven't gone so far as to buy a telescope or anything like that, but I find myself staring up at it a lot."

"Still certain you'll see the man in the moon?"

She snickered. "Yes."

One night he had brought her up here and she'd been convinced that if she kept looking hard enough then she would see the man in the moon. It had all been in jest, the kind of fun they'd enjoyed together. They'd shared all their secrets…even the silly ones. Later they had made love in the backseat of his car. "Let's sit down on the steps."

Other than the sound of crickets chirping, the night was quiet. There was a gentle breeze coming off the mountains, twirling around the canyons and valleys. He had a feeling it would rain later in the week. He could deal with any kind of weather, other than a heavy snowstorm. All Westmorelands detested snow, except for Riley. His brother actually looked forward to blizzards.

Canyon glanced over at Keisha. He hadn't allowed himself to think that one day she would return to Denver and sit beside him under his sky again. Underneath Flash. But she was here. Now if she could only get beyond the hurt and anger she felt were justified.

She was leaning back on her arms and staring up at the sky. What she was thinking? How she was feeling? There had been so much animosity between them, but he hoped they could continue to find common ground without hostility and bitterness, for their son's sake.

"What are you thinking?" he decided to ask her.

When she glanced over at him he saw a semblance of regret in her eyes. "I was thinking of how things could have been."

If you hadn't screwed up, he figured she didn't add. He

was fully aware that she still placed the blame for their three-year separation at his feet, but it wasn't justified. However, he refused to think about that tonight. "Sometimes it's best not to go back, Keisha. The best plan of action is to let go and move on."

"Is it?"

He gave her a tight smile. "I think so. It's a matter of forgiveness on all accounts…especially if it's a past you can't change."

She arched her brow, but didn't say anything as she stared at him. He knew how that analytical mind of hers worked. She assumed he was hinting that she should forgive him…but that was far from the truth. As far as he was concerned he hadn't done anything that needed to be forgiven. And to give himself credit, unlike Zane who hadn't tried getting Channing back when she left town, Canyon had done everything he'd known how to do to get Keisha back.

He figured she had run home to her mother in Texas, and he had tried calling but she'd changed her cell phone number. He'd even gone to see Bonita and pleaded with her to contact Keisha and tell her the truth but she'd refused. Bonita wouldn't even tell him why she had blatantly lied about the entire situation. And when he had sought out Bonita's ex, to see if Grant could shed light on why Bonita had done what she'd done, he'd only learned that Grant had moved away.

Finally, bitterness and resentment had settled in and he'd decided that if Keisha assumed the worst about him so be it. He would not try to run her down and plead his innocence. If she didn't trust him, then he was better off without her.

But then she had come back to town. As far as he was concerned, her return had been a game changer. Especially since he'd found out she'd given birth to his son. Now he couldn't help raising his hand and smoothing out the frown that had settled around her brow.

"What are you doing?" she asked in a quiet tone.

He smiled. "You're working yourself into another headache by thinking too much, about all the wrong things."

"Am I?"

"Yes."

Several moments of silence hovered between them. He felt it, that physical chemistry that was always there. They could try to ignore it, try to put a cap on it or they could give in to it. No need to think it would ever get out of their system because that wasn't possible. No matter the time or the situation, he would always want Keisha.

He felt the pounding in his heart and, of their own accord, his fingers moved from her brow, brushing a lock of hair from her face before slowly sliding down to her lips. The tips of his fingers grazed softly across her mouth, and he heard the breathless sigh in her throat when her lips parted.

Old habits die hard. In the past, whenever her lips would part on a breathless sigh, he'd known just what to do about it. The same thing he was about to do now.

Shifting his position, his arms slid around her waist as he lowered his head and took her mouth with a possession that rocked him to the core.

Acting on instinct and insatiable hunger, Keisha's tongue mated passionately with Canyon's. For now, she was willing to do what he suggested, let go and move on. And she refused to question why something she'd thought impossible was now feasible. Canyon made sure she continued not to question by kissing her such that her yearning for him came back into focus. Her desire for him manipulated her emotions in a way she couldn't combat. He was reducing her to a ball of urgency and need. An entreaty for more escalated through her. He deepened the kiss, taking control of her mouth with firm strokes, making even more intense moans flow from deep within her throat.

Canyon stood and drew her up with him, not breaking their kiss. His hands moved to her backside and eased her closer to the fit of him, flexing his hips against her. She could feel the hardness of his erection, pressing against the juncture of her thighs, triggering more greed within her. It was a greed she'd kept dormant for three years, and the slow yet urgent strokes of his tongue were bringing that greed back to life.

He slowly pulled his mouth from hers and she knew the need to breathe was the only reason he'd broken off the kiss. She saw how his handsome face was bathed in the moonlight and the way his gaze held hers hostage while her body churned and blood rushed hotly through her veins.

Suddenly, as if neither of them could withstand the lust overtaking them, Canyon swept her into his arms and carried her back into the house and upstairs to his bedroom.

No man should want a woman this much, Canyon thought, putting Keisha down. She looked like a tempting miniature morsel in the ocean of covers on his huge bed.

While he watched, she scampered to her knees to remove her robe and then her nightshirt. He couldn't help but stand and watch her undress. When she had tossed aside the last piece of clothing, leaving her naked and totally exposed, the bulge in his pajama bottoms hardened, swelling to gigantic proportions.

When she eased up, stretching her body, she showcased a pair of firm breasts, a small waist, a flat stomach and curvy hips. His gaze dipped lower to the juncture of her thighs and his mouth watered.

Growling with primitive savagery and a feverish hunger, he eased his bottoms down his thighs as his gaze remained focused on her. He knew every measure of that body. Had touched it. Tasted it. Devoured it. Emotions clogged his throat when he saw where her interest lay as he stood before her totally naked.

"You're still the Grand Canyon, I see."

He couldn't help the smile that spread across his lips. At that moment, it didn't matter what she believed or didn't believe. Tonight his sheets would get scorched to oblivion when he made love to her. "Glad you think so."

He moved over to the bed and joined her, pulling her into his arms and easing her onto her back against the pillows, intending to lick every inch of her skin, starting at her lips. He whispered, "I missed you and I intend to show you how much."

And then he began his feast, holding her hips when she squirmed in pleasure beneath his mouth. By the time his tongue reached her breasts and supped on the protruding nipples, he felt them harden even more in his mouth. She called out his name but he only continued his sensuous assault, determined to remind her how good they were together and what they had once meant to each other.

Keisha shuddered with sensations as Canyon's mouth moved across her body, leaving no area untouched. His hand moved from her hips and drifted lower. She gasped at the feel of his fingers settling between her legs, sliding through her curls. At the same time, his mouth licked circles around her naval, causing a moan to rise in her throat.

And just when she thought there was no way she could take any more, he parted her womanly folds, slid a finger inside of her and began stroking her intimately. No woman could survive his skillful hand and she closed her eyes against the sensual torture.

Moments later, when she felt his tongue replace his finger, her eyes flew open. "Canyon!"

If he heard her scream his name he didn't let on, instead he deepened the kiss and intensified her agony, stroking his tongue in the right places, using his hands to lift her hips off the bed to get his mouth closer to her. Every nerve ending in her body strummed with intense pleasure.

Her body jerked when an orgasm tore through her and she screamed his name again and again. When the last spasm left her body, she slowly opened her eyes and watched Canyon reach into the nightstand and pull out a condom pack. He quickly sheathed himself, eased his body over hers and gazed down at her, his eyes filled with absolute possession and passion.

"Look at me, Keisha," he said in a low command. "Look at me and see the man I am, the man you've always known. One day you'll know that I could not have betrayed you. Not when I have loved you from day one. Not when after all that's happened between us, I still love you."

She held his gaze and her heart pounded. And as she read the truth in his eyes, she felt her own fill with tears. Because she knew at that moment she had been wrong. "Oh, Canyon…"

He leaned down, licking the tears that flowed down her cheeks before taking her mouth in another ferocious kiss. Cupping her hips, he lifted her and entered her in one long, hard thrust, going deep, all the way to the hilt. And then he began moving, stroking, thrusting in and out—making love to her with an intensity that snatched her breath from her lungs.

Lifting her legs, she wrapped them around his waist,

tightening them in a firm grip as another orgasm ripped through her. She knew the exact moment the pinnacle of a climax consumed him, as well. He released her mouth and threw his head back. His growl permeated the air as he continued to stroke deep inside of her.

Then his mouth returned to hers and blood surged through her veins. He kissed her with an intensity that made her shiver inside. Moments later, he released her mouth and she whispered, "I'm sorry," in a broken tone. "I am so sorry."

He cupped her face in his hands, kissed the side of her lips and said softly, "I accept your apology, sweetheart."

Canyon wasn't sure why he awoke in the middle of the night. But when he opened his eyes and shifted in bed the clock on the nightstand indicated it was almost four in the morning. And the spot beside him was empty. He would have thought he'd dreamed last night had it not been for Keisha's feminine scent that was infused in his bedcovers.

When he heard a sob, he glanced over at his bedroom window. Keisha stood there, staring out into the night. She was crying. Concern tugged at his heart and he slid out of bed, walked over and put his arms around her. As if she needed his strength, she turned in his arms and buried her face in his chest, wetting his skin with her tears.

He tightened his arms around her. "Shh. Don't cry. It's okay. It doesn't matter anymore."

She pulled out of his arms and looked up at him with tearstained eyes. "Why did she lie, Canyon? Why did she deliberately tear us apart?"

He pulled her to him and wrapped his arms around her again. "The only person who could answer that is Bonita, sweetheart. Unfortunately, she took the reason to the grave with her. We might never know."

She tossed her head back and looked up at him. "How?"

He lifted a brow. "How?"

"Yes, how can you stand the sight of me after all I did, all I said and believed? How can you forgive me when I'm having a difficult time forgiving myself? How can you think you love me?"

Canyon sighed deeply while tracing a path up and down her back with his hands. He wondered what he could say to help her understand. "I was hurt and angry for a long time, Keisha. I convinced myself that I hated you for what you did to us. And then when I found out about Beau, and realized what you've deliberately denied me for two years, I became furious." He paused. "But Dillon made me realize a few things."

"What?"

"First, that you had a choice. You didn't have to keep Beau when you found out you were pregnant. You hated me and thought I had betrayed you. He was a reminder of what you thought I did. Yet you chose to have him and for that I am grateful. And Dillon made me see that if the roles had been reversed, and I had come home to find another man in bed with you coming out of the bathroom in just a towel, I would have thought the worst, as well."

"But Bonita lied through her teeth. She intentionally wanted me to believe the worst about you."

And you did. He forced that thought to the back of his mind. "Doesn't matter, you know the truth now. I had convinced myself I didn't love you. I even thought I hated you at one time. But all it took was kissing you, holding you in my arms and making love to you to show me what my true emotions were. I discovered the truth that there is a thin line between love and hate."

Not giving her a chance to say anything, he swept her off her feet and into his arms. He carried her over to the bed.

"I checked on Beau, and he's sleeping peacefully," she said, looking at him.

"Good, because for the next hour, you won't be." Then he captured her mouth with his.

Eleven

The next morning, Keisha rushed downstairs. She had woken up in Canyon's bed and upon realizing how late it was—after eight already—she'd quickly slid back into her nightgown, grabbed her robe and fled from the room. Beau was an early riser, and from the moment he opened his eyes, he could be a force to reckon with. He was at that age where he assumed food should be at his beck and call.

As she rounded the corner leading to the kitchen she heard voices. Canyon was standing at the counter sipping a cup of coffee while Beau sat at the kitchen table eating eggs, bacon and toast, and drinking milk while talking nonstop, telling Canyon about the *big* horse he wanted.

When he detected her presence, Canyon turned sensual dark eyes on her. Immediately, her nipples puckered beneath the robe, the juncture of her thighs tingled and shivers of desire raced through her. After a full night of hot-and-heavy lovemaking, one would think sex would be the last thing on her mind this morning. But it wasn't. And from the look in Canyon's eyes, it wasn't the last thing on his mind either.

"Good morning, Keisha," he said in a voice singed with a sexiness.

She swallowed. "Good morning." She then moved to the table and kissed the tip of Beau's nose. "And how are you, Beau?"

Beau smiled. "Beau good. Food good. Daddy-Dad good, too."

Keisha chuckled. *Yes, Daddy-Dad is definitely good. Better than good,* she thought. She had indulged in hours and hours of lovemaking last night and he had proved that he hadn't lost his edge. In the bedroom, Canyon Westmoreland was still the best. She glanced down at Beau's plate. It seemed Canyon had also improved his cooking skills since the last time they'd been together.

She glanced up at him. "You did a good job dressing him."

Canyon smiled and his dimple oozed with rich sensuality. "I've been getting a lot of practice with Denver. I've been known to babysit a time or two."

She nodded. "And who taught you how to cook?"

His smile widened. "Chloe. When Ramsey's cook Nellie decided to move away last year, Chloe took on all the cooking for Ramsey and his men and let Lucia run the magazine company. Chloe enjoys getting up at the crack of dawn and the men loved her cooking and enjoyed seeing her pretty face in the morning.

"Chloe also felt all the single Westmorelands without cooking skills could benefit from a basic cooking class. Ramsey and Dillon seconded that notion, so now I can fend for myself."

He moved away from the counter and pulled her into his arms. "Now to kiss you good-morning properly."

By the time he released her mouth, Keisha was weak in the knees.

"Daddy-Dad, you bit Mommy!" Beau exclaimed.

Canyon chuckled as he rubbed the top of his son's curly head. "No, Beau, I *kissed* Mommy. You're going to see a lot of that around here."

Keisha swallowed. Canyon had said it as if he expected her to be hanging around a lot. Maybe this was not the time to tell him that although she now knew how wrong she'd been about him and he had admitted to still loving her, she couldn't rush into anything. She still had to return to her home when the seven days were up. She and Canyon needed to restart their relationship but rushing into things was not the way to do it. They had a lot of history to work through. They should take things one day at a time.

"Eat up, Beau. Aunt Pam is on her way."

She glanced up at Canyon. "Pam is coming for Beau?"

"Yes. We have a lot of business to take care of this morning, and I called and asked if she'd mind watching Beau. She thought it was a wonderful idea. The other day Beau and Denver played well together."

"Yes, but she has one in diapers. Three might be a lot for her to handle."

"Not for Pam. Dade isn't walking yet so he doesn't get in as much trouble. She mentioned that Chloe would be coming over later with Susan and Rembrandt and they plan on making it a fun day for the kids."

"Oh."

Canyon didn't say anything for a long moment. He just stood there studying her with intense eyes. Finally he asked, "You don't have a problem with the plans I made for Beau today, do you?"

A part of her did. She hoped she could make him understand. "I'm just used to making decisions about Beau on my own. Before, it's just been me and him."

He nodded. "I understand, but now there's the three of us. And if I ever do anything you don't agree with or that you're not comfortable with, let me know."

Keisha knew she was being silly. There wasn't a single mother out there who wouldn't want the father of her child to take an active role…especially if that role was a good one. And there was no doubt in her mind that Canyon and his family would be good for Beau.

"Keisha?"

She saw the concern in his eyes. "No problem. I'll just go upstairs and change. What time are we meeting with the attorney?"

"At noon. But I need to take you home first to get Beau's birth certificate."

"All right. I'll go upstairs and get dressed and be right back."

She was quiet, Canyon thought, glancing over at Keisha. They were in his car, on their way to her place and she hadn't said much. Keisha had been okay when Pam had arrived for Beau, but it seemed that once they'd driven away from Westmoreland Country, she'd withdrawn into her own thoughts.

He'd been trying to keep the conversation going by talking about the man who'd been elected mayor of Denver during the time she'd been gone, and what a great job the guy was doing. He'd even brought her up to date on his great-grandfather Raphel and how Megan's husband, Rico, was involved in investigating his great-grandfather's past. It seemed Raphel had been involved with other women before marrying their great-grandmother, and one of those women had borne him a child. That meant they could have more cousins out there somewhere. Westmorelands were big on family and they hoped Rico's investigation would shed light on who those cousins were and where they were now.

"You okay?" he asked her.

She glanced over at him. "Yes, I'm fine. Just feeling a little disgusted again about my house and the condition it's in, and worried because the police are still clueless about who did it."

He heard the frustration in her tone and understood it. He hadn't mentioned that he'd spoken to Pete this morning because there hadn't been anything new to report. "Well, I think we have the best police force around, if that makes you feel any better," he said, reaching over to take her hand in his when they came to a traffic light.

A small smile touched her lips. "I'll take your word for it."

His hand returned to the steering wheel when the traffic light changed. "So tell me how your mom is doing. Is she still a radiologist at that hospital?"

"Yes, and she doesn't plan to retire anytime soon." She then told him about her mother's breast cancer scare and how she was glad she had been with her during that time. "She took a leave of absence when Beau was born because she refused to let anyone else keep him while he was so young," she added. "So she kept him for eight months, and I appreciated it." She paused a moment and then said softly, "I think she might be seeing my father again."

Canyon was certain if he hadn't needed to come to a stop at another traffic light, he might have slammed on his breaks anyway. He looked over at her. "Your mother and your old man?"

"The man who got her pregnant? Yes," she clarified.

She drew in a deep breath and then added, "I never told you this, but my father saw me when I was fifteen. It was then that he realized my mother hadn't lied after all."

No, Canyon thought. She'd never told him that. In fact, she'd only told him how the man had denied the baby was his when her mother had told him about her pregnancy. "So what did he do when he realized you were his child?"

"He tried making up for lost time, but it was too late. I knew the whole story of how he'd broken my mother's heart, and I decided that I didn't want to have anything to do with him."

So in other words, Canyon thought, she had totally dismissed her father and kept him out of her life—just like she'd done with him. "So what makes you think your mother has hooked back up with him after all this time?"

"Because as I got older I realized something."

"What?"

"That she never dated another man. She had friends and work, but she made me her life. For years I just assumed she enjoyed being independent, but now I can see things differently. She was hurt by his rejection, which is why we moved away from Texas. But now I believe the reason she never dated is because she couldn't give her heart to another man."

Canyon didn't say anything. What she said was probably true because he'd once walked that same road. When Keisha had left Denver believing the worst about him, he'd been hurt and it had taken him a while to get back into the dating scene. But even then he'd known he would never love another woman the way he'd loved her.

"And lately," Keisha said, breaking into his thoughts. "She's been bringing him up each and every time we talk. It was subtle at first but now she's been trying to convince me that he regrets not accepting me as his, he regrets turning his back on me for the first fifteen years of my life."

He imagined that wasn't going over well with her since she tended to see things as black or white. "How do you feel about that? About your mom getting back with him?" he asked.

She shrugged. "I want to think I have no feelings one way or the other. It's her life. However, I don't understand how she can be so forgiving."

"Why? Because you wouldn't be so forgiving?" he asked, trying to keep his voice calm when frankly, he was getting annoyed with her attitude. "In that case, it's a good thing that you thought I betrayed you and not the other way around."

At her confused look he explained, "If I had been the one seeking your forgiveness because I mistakenly thought you betrayed me, chances are I wouldn't have gotten it."

Canyon's words left Keisha speechless. What could she say? Her own mother had made a similar assertion to her yesterday. Okay, she would admit that forgiving didn't come easily for her. And she would even concede that her inability to forgive easily was the reason she'd kept Beau from his father for two years. However, she'd been wrong to go that far and had admitted that, asking for Canyon's forgiveness. And he had forgiven her. Was she being too hard on her father? Did he deserve to be forgiven like she had been?

"We're here."

She snapped out of her reverie and glanced around. They had pulled up in her driveway and there were several vans already parked there. "What's going on?" she asked, already opening the door to get out.

"The cleaning team I hired is here."

When she reached his side, she turned to him with a look of surprise on her face. "You hired a cleaning team?"

"Yes. I had to talk Pete into giving me your key and he only did so after I told him what I planned to do. I didn't want you to worry about cleaning up the place and it had to get done. A few years ago there was a fire at the home Bella inherited from her grandfather. This same company came in and did an awesome job, so I figured they could do the same here. I contacted them Saturday and I think you're going to be pleased."

Keisha couldn't say anything. Saturday hadn't been a good day for them and they hadn't been on the best of terms. Yet he had cared enough to hire some company to come in and get her house back in order. She took his hand in hers and held his gaze. "Thank you."

She meant it more than he would ever know. She hadn't looked forward to coming here today, knowing what she would find. But he'd been kind enough to take care of it for her.

"You're welcome." He tightened his hand on hers. "Come on, let me introduce you to everyone."

Keisha met the owners of the company—Mr. and Mrs. Helton—and their crew. From the moment she'd walked over the threshold she'd seen firsthand what a great job they'd done. Already they had righted her house to the extent that she couldn't tell it had been trashed. A new coat of paint had been applied to her walls and new carpeting had been installed throughout the house. All of the colors matched her original interior design choices. The kitchen was spotless and the floor tile was a gleaming white. She thought her house looked better now than it had before.

"The clothes that were thrown all over your floors have been taken to the cleaners or have been washed," Mrs. Helton said. "Are you pleased, Ms. Ashford?"

"Yes," Keisha said without hesitation. She glanced around her bedroom, amazed. A new coverlet and new fluffy pillows were on her bed. The new carpeting, a shade of tan darker than what had been there before, was the perfect blend. She'd seen Beau's room and her office and those rooms looked incredible, as well. "Your company did a fantastic job."

The woman beamed. "Thanks. Mr. Westmoreland said to make it special for you because you were special."

Keisha glanced over to where Canyon stood in the hallway, talking with Mr. Helton. "Well, you followed his instructions by doing an outstanding job."

"Thank you. Unless there's something else you think we need to do, we'll be leaving now."

Keisha nodded. "No, everything looks great."

The woman nodded with a smile on her face. "If you see anything we've missed after we leave, just give us a call. Our card is on your dresser and another on your kitchen counter."

"Thanks, I will."

The woman left and Keisha went into her bathroom and marveled at the new set of towels, matching throw rugs and shower curtain. A beautiful vase of artificial spring flowers that looked so real—she leaned down to sniff to make sure they weren't—looked perfect sitting on the new vanity.

"Keisha?"

"Coming," she said, leaving the bathroom to find Canyon standing in the middle of her bedroom. Did he always have to look so good? Have so much testosterone oozing from every pore? Her heart began pounding like crazy in her chest as she slid her gaze over the full length of him.

"Looks good, doesn't it?"

"Most definitely," she said, fully realizing they were talking about two different things.

He looked at her and smiled. "I'm glad you're pleased."

"I definitely am. However, I might have bad memories of how this place looked, unless…"

He raised a thick dark brow. "Unless what?"

She didn't say anything for a moment while toe-curling desire trickled through her. And then she moved, walking over to stand in front of him. "Unless the bad memories are replaced with good ones."

No one could credit Canyon with being slow. But then it could have been the way her hardened nipples pressed against her shirt that gave her away. He took a step closer and wrapped his arms around her waist. "Need my help doing that? Replacing those memories?"

She leaned in closer to him. "Are you volunteering, Canyon?"

"Yes, I'm volunteering."

She nibbled on her bottom lip. "Do we have time? There is that matter of our appointment with an attorney at noon."

"We'll make time."

Pulling his cell phone out of his pocket, he punched in some numbers without taking his eyes off her. Moments later he said into the phone, "Hey, this is Canyon. We're running late, Roy."

There was a pause and then. "How late?" He smiled down at Keisha as he continued to speak into the phone. "At least a couple of hours. Maybe three." Then, "Fine. We'll see you then." He clicked off the phone and slid it back into his pocket.

Keisha felt her pulse beat wildly near her throat. "The front door?"

"Locked."

She sighed in anticipation. She knew that look in his

eyes. It had been there each and every time he'd made love to her.

He cupped her face between strong hands, leaned closer and whispered huskily, "I want you."

She whispered back, "And I want you."

Within seconds, his hungry mouth was devouring hers, mating with her tongue like he owned it. Possessing it. Claiming it. All in the sweep of his tongue as he took her mouth with a skill that was all consuming. No other man could make a kiss so stimulating and erotic. A moan of lust she couldn't contain forced its way out of her throat.

With their mouths still locked together, he backed her toward the bed. When they reached their destination, he lifted his mouth from hers and began removing her clothes. Lifting her blouse over her head, he proceeded to slide her skirt down her hips. She was left in only her bra and panties. He reached behind her and unhooked her bra. Eager, he cupped the twin globes of her breasts in his hands, his fingers brushing across the nipples. As though on cue, her body flamed at the juncture of her legs and she moaned deep within her throat.

Then he released her breasts, crouched down on his haunches and pressed his face to her feminine mound and drew in her scent.

Keisha knew what he planned to do, and when he licked her through the silk of her panties, she tightened her hands on his shoulders. "Canyon," she said, whispering his name on a shivering moan.

Canyon pulled back to ease Keisha's panties down her legs, barely able to contain his hunger. Before she could take her next breath, he parted her feminine folds and put his tongue inside her.

One of the things he'd missed most was this. Her deli-

cious taste. She trembled hard and he held her firmly by
her hips, intending to have his fill and give her pleasure.
Over and over, he flicked his tongue over her and lapped
up the taste of honey.

She moaned and arched forward. He continued to hold
her hips as he felt pleasure ripple through her, making her
say his name. The sound infiltrated his brain, intoxicated
his soul and whipped him with just as much pleasure as
it seemed she was feeling. When the last tremble passed
through her, he slowly stood, gathered her close and then
tumbled her down on the bed with him.

"You still have your clothes on," Keisha mumbled, when
he slid off her to stand by the bed.

"Something I'm about to remedy," he said, pulling his
belt through the loops of his jeans.

She rested against one of the huge pillows and watched
him while aftershocks of pleasure strummed through her.
With her gaze glued to his body, she watched him undress.
First his shirt. "Mmm," she said as he eased his jeans
down his legs along with his briefs. The man was so well
endowed. "It's always nice to revisit the Grand Canyon."

"Glad you want to," he said in a deep, sexy voice.

"Oh, I do."

After sheathing himself with a condom he'd taken from
his wallet, he returned to the bed. When his knees touched
the mattress, he dipped his head and brought his mouth
straight to her mouth, mating with it in slow easy strokes.
Moments later, breaking the kiss, he pulled her to him,
placing her back to his chest.

A shiver of anticipation stirred through her. There had
never been a dull moment with Canyon in the bedroom
and she had a feeling he was about to reacquaint her with
some of those times.

After pushing her up to her hands and knees and turning her to face the headboard, she felt him caress the contours of her back, thighs and backside. She sucked in her breath when his fingers eased between her legs and found her wetness. Then he replaced his hands with feathery kisses.

When she thought she couldn't handle it anymore, he mounted her from behind, sliding into her, clamping her back to his front, thrusting in and out of her with slow, measured strokes. She closed her eyes, wondering if she would survive all the pleasure.

And then the tempo changed. He pounded into her harder, faster, while stroking his hands over her breasts. The sound of flesh slapping against flesh pervaded the air and she couldn't help but moan. Her muscles, greedy for his invasion, clinched tight with each inward thrust.

A shiver began in the pit of her stomach and spread. She tried forcing it back, not ready for an explosion just yet. Not wanting this to end. Her body was ready, but she wasn't. She wanted to go on and on, and enjoy each powerful thrust.

"Let go, baby," Canyon whispered close to her ear as he increased the tempo even more. "I won't let go until you do and the pleasure is killing me," he muttered the words in a savage growl.

She let go. Screaming at the top of her lungs while he rode her hard, their bodies locked together. He let out one hell of a sensuous snarl, before roaring out her name. Moments later, as they tumbled down in the bed, he gathered her close.

She felt the aftershocks leave his body and hers and knew it would be a while before either of them had the energy to move.

Twelve

"Glad the two of you were finally able to make it."

Keisha nervously nibbled her bottom lip, totally embarrassed. Their appointment had been at noon and it was now four o'clock. She and Canyon were sitting next to each other, across from the man's huge desk. "Sorry, we're late, Mr. McDonald."

Canyon muttered softly, "I'm not."

She gave him a warning look and hoped Roy McDonald hadn't heard what he'd said. She felt bad all the way around. She'd even called Pam and apologized. After telling Pam this morning that they would be by to get Beau before two o'clock, they were late for that, as well. Pam had understood and told her not to worry. Beau was fine and was having fun with Denver. Pam had even suggested that she and Canyon grab something to eat while they were out because Beau could eat dinner with Denver.

"You did bring the birth certificate with you so we can start the paperwork?"

"Yes," she said, handing him the document. Roy McDonald appeared to be in his mid-fifties and, according to Canyon, he had handled business for the Westmorelands for a number of years.

She studied the bracelet on her wrist so she wouldn't be tempted to look over at Canyon. The last thing she needed to remember was what had happened back at her house. Not once, but twice. To say her home was now filled with good memories was an understatement.

"Well, the paperwork will be easier than I thought. All I need is your signature on a piece of documentation, Canyon."

Canyon lifted a brow. "Why will it be so easy?" he asked.

"Because you're already showing as Beau Ashford's biological father on his birth certificate, so all I'm doing is a simple name change."

"What?" He turned to Keisha, confused. "You listed me as Beau's father?"

Keisha nodded slowly. "Yes."

"Why?"

Roy McDonald didn't understand Canyon's question and interrupted to ask. "The child isn't yours?"

Canyon frowned at Roy. "Of course he's mine. What makes you think otherwise?"

Roy shrugged. "By the nature of the question you just asked Ms. Ashford."

Canyon drew in a deep breath. "I'm not asking because I think Beau isn't mine, I'm asking because I'm surprised she would have acknowledged it that way."

"Oh." Roy then stood and headed for the door.

"Where are you going?" Canyon asked.

Roy turned around and smiled. "To the break room to watch CNN. Evidently the two of you need to talk about a few things without me." He then left, closing the door behind him.

Canyon turned his attention back to Keisha. "Why?"

She nervously nibbled her bottom lip. "Mom always said that was the one thing she regretted not doing, naming my father on my birth certificate. If anything had happened to her I would not have known anything about him. I didn't want that for Beau in case he wanted to find you someday."

He nodded. "Thank you for doing that."

"You don't have to thank me."

"Yes," he said, standing and pulling her up from her chair, as well. "I do."

Then he kissed her with an appreciation he felt in every cell of his body. Last night and this afternoon had proved that their three-year separation hadn't eradicated the passion between them. If anything, their passion was more intense than ever. It wouldn't take much for him to place her on Roy's desk and take her here and now. Kissing her with slow thoroughness had a way of making him lose control.

There was a quick knock on the door and Roy stuck his head in. "I take it we're going to proceed as planned."

Canyon chuckled. "Yes, that wasn't the issue, Roy."

Roy lifted a brow as he returned to his desk. "Then what was the issue?"

Smiling, Canyon continued to hold Keisha's hand as they returned to their seats. "It doesn't matter anymore. From here on out, we're moving forward."

"Welcome to McKays. Will there be just the two of you dining this evening, Mr. Westmoreland?" the waitress asked.

"Yes, Priscilla, just the two of us."

Smiling, Priscilla said, "Then please follow me," as she led them to a table that had a gorgeous view of the mountains.

Once seated, Keisha glanced over at Canyon. "Are you sure it's okay for us to take time to eat here? I would have been okay if we had grabbed something from one of those fast-food places. I'd hate for Pam to think we're taking advantage of her kindness with Beau."

Canyon shook his head, grinning. "Believe me, no one in my family will ever think that. Besides, it's a way for Beau to start getting to know everyone since they'll become a vital part of his life."

Keisha took a sip of the water the server placed in front of them, deciding not to ask what he meant by that. However, eventually she and Canyon would have to talk. More than once today he'd hinted at something permanent between them as if it was a done deal. And it wasn't. Although he was willing to leave the past behind them and move ahead, she wasn't sure she could do it so easily. There were still some things she needed to work through—specifically, her guilt.

She had accused him wrongly, which had resulted in her treating him unjustly. And whenever she thought about what he had missed out on, what Beau had missed out on… she could only lay the blame at her own feet. He might be willing to forgive her, but forgiveness had never come easy to her. This time, it was *herself* she wasn't sure she could forgive. Her actions had cost him two years of his son's life. It had cost her three years of anger and pain that she'd let fester inside of her for no reason. Before she could consider getting back together with Canyon, she had to figure out her own issues.

Moments later, after the server came back to give them

menus, Canyon said, "I think I'm going to order us a bottle of champagne."

She raised a brow. "Why?"

"Because we have reasons to celebrate. We have a son and we're moving forward—"

"It's nice running into you two."

Keisha glanced up and stared into the face of Grant Palmer.

Canyon stood. He wasn't sure what lie Bonita might have told Grant about that night three years ago. If the man planned to make a scene, then Canyon was ready. He'd only met Grant once before, and that was when he had accompanied Keisha to a birthday bash Bonita had given her fiancé. "Grant. You're back in Denver?"

"Only for a short while. I flew in this weekend to attend a cousin's wedding," Grant said, smiling and offering Canyon his hand in a hearty handshake.

Canyon knew his surprise showed on his face as he accepted the man's hand. Grant wasn't acting like someone holding a grudge. When Canyon glanced over at Keisha he could tell she was just as baffled as he was.

It was Grant's next statement that muddied the waters even more. "I'm glad the two of you are back together and relieved Bonita was able to make things right with you before she died."

Canyon glanced over at Keisha who had a *what is he talking about* look on her face. Keisha asked, "What do you mean, Grant?"

"I mean what happened that night…when it looked as if Bonita and Canyon had slept together."

Canyon felt as if he'd just been delivered a sucker punch to the gut. "You knew it wasn't true?" Canyon asked in an incredulous tone that had a bit of a bite to it.

Grant's smile faded. "Yes." He glanced at Keisha. "Didn't she explain everything? She said she would."

Canyon shook his head, wondering what the hell was going on here. Before he could ask Grant to elaborate, Keisha spoke up with a slight tremor in her voice. "Bonita didn't explain anything to me, Grant. But Canyon and I would be most appreciative if you would."

Grant joined them after telling the friends he was dining with that he would rejoin them later. After Canyon told their waitress they weren't ready to order their meals but did want to order Grant a drink, a perplexed Grant sat down and said, "I think I'll start from the beginning."

"Please do," Keisha encouraged, smiling. She knew Canyon was just as bewildered as she was.

"It was the night I broke off our engagement," Grant said.

"You had broken off your engagement that night," Keisha repeated his words in surprise.

"Yes. I found out some disturbing news about Bonita." He paused when the waitress placed his drink in front of him. "She had a split personality." He paused. "In her dominant personality, she was the woman I fell in love with and wanted to marry, but in her subordinate one, she was a totally different person."

"When did you find out about her two personalities?" Canyon asked.

"Not soon enough. The reason I broke off with her is because I found out the other Bonita was having an affair with another man. The wife suspected something and had a video camera installed in her home. It showed Bonita and the man together one weekend while the wife was out of town. It was filmed two weeks after we'd become engaged but, according to the wife, the affair had been going on for quite some time."

He didn't say anything else for a minute. After taking a sip of his drink, he continued, "When she came home from work, I confronted her and she denied it, claimed it wasn't her. But it *was* her. I had already gone through her drawers and found stuff I'd never seen before. All kinds of sex toys and crap. I even found her journal, which pretty much corroborated the wife's story about how long the affair had been going on. When I explained all of that, Bonita burst into tears and denied everything."

Grant paused again. "I didn't believe her and moved out that night, told her the engagement was off and I never wanted to see her again. And I didn't. But then two years later she showed up in Florida at the college where I'm teaching. That's when she told me the truth about her split personalities and that she was getting treatment from a mental-health professional. It was then that she confessed to what she'd done to you—at least what the other Bonita had done to you—the night I broke off our engagement."

"And what did she tell you?" Keisha asked quietly.

"She told me how the dominant Bonita was upset, distraught over our broken engagement. She drove across town to see you, Keisha, needing a friend, a shoulder to cry on because she couldn't understand how I could accuse her of such things. She said it was only after Canyon came to the door that she remembered you were out of town. He saw how distraught Bonita was, let her in, offered her something to drink and even shared a drink with her."

"I take it she had no memory of changing roles?" Canyon asked.

Grant shook his head sadly. "No. None. Although she saw the video of her affair for herself she denied knowl-

edge of any of it. She even claimed those items and the
journal weren't hers."

Grant took another sip of his drink before continuing.
"She said she was fine at first…the normal Bonita. But
then after Canyon excused himself to go take a shower
that's when the other Bonita emerged. She's the one who
undressed and got into your bed with plans to seduce Canyon when he finished with his shower. The only thing was,
he walked out of the shower the minute you walked into
the bedroom, Keisha. And you assumed you had caught
Bonita and Canyon in an illicit act."

Keisha found Canyon staring at her with penetrating
dark eyes. She didn't have to imagine what he was thinking. The shame of guilt was more powerful than ever. She
could clearly recall that night, how he had pleaded with
her to believe him and how Bonita had pleaded with her
not to believe him. Keisha had been so hell-bent on believing the worst that she hadn't taken the time to notice
that Bonita's behavior was different. Keisha had said some
god-awful things to the both of them, told them they had
better be out of her place before she came back. She had
specifically told Canyon to clear everything he owned out
and not to try to contact her or else she would put a restraining order in place. She had ended up driving to the
mall and sitting in the parking lot in her car for hours just
crying. By the time she had returned home all traces of
Canyon were gone.

She never saw Bonita alive after that night, and she
had refused to take Canyon's calls. She'd even changed
her phone number. She had heard Bonita and Grant had
ended their engagement, and she'd assumed he'd found
out what had happened. Less than two weeks later, hurt,
alone and pregnant, she had resigned from her job and
moved back to Texas.

Drawing in a deep breath, Keisha asked softly, "When did Bonita realize there were two of her?"

"Not until she was arrested for shoplifting."

"My God," Keisha said, her hand flying to her chest in shock.

"The court required that she receive mental-health treatment and she did. When she realized the full impact of what she'd done to us, and to you, Keisha, the two people she had trusted the most and who had trusted her, she was devastated. That's why she came to see me in Florida and why she had planned to fly to see you in Texas. I assumed she had when I saw you and Canyon together.

"I guess she was killed before she had a chance to tell you anything. Her mother mentioned you attended the memorial services, so I assumed Bonita had confided in you, told you the truth, and that you had forgiven her. Had I known that wasn't the case and that you were still under the assumption that Canyon had betrayed you, I would have made it my business to make sure you both knew the truth."

Keisha nodded. "I went to her funeral out of respect for her family and noticed you weren't there," she said.

Grant ran a frustrated hand down his face. "No, I couldn't make myself go and see her that way. A part of me felt that I had failed her. I thought the worst of her but had I known the extent of her mental illness, I would have forgiven her and gotten her help. But I didn't know," he said brokenly.

Keisha didn't say anything because, at that moment, she felt as if she had failed Bonita, as well.

Canyon woke up for the second night in a row and found the spot beside him empty. Pulling himself up in bed he ran a hand down his face before glancing over at the window where he knew Keisha would be. She was standing in front of it, staring up at the sky like she'd done the night before.

Once Grant had left to rejoin his friends, the mood for celebrating with champagne had vanished. Instead they had ordered dinner and exchanged few words. He figured both of them were wondering if there was some way they could have detected Bonita's mental condition and he was sure there wasn't.

But he had a feeling Keisha believed otherwise. Keisha and Bonita had been good friends, and a part of Canyon was saddened about how the friendship had ended. But the last thing he would let Keisha think was that what had happened with Bonita was her fault. Easing out of bed he walked behind her and wrapped his arms around her, drawing her close to his solid chest.

"I didn't mean to wake you," she whispered.

"You didn't. I woke up and found you gone. Now that I have you back in my bed it's hard for me to think of you not being there with me." When she didn't say anything, he tightened his arms around her. "Talk to me, Keisha. Share your thoughts."

He heard her deep sigh. "I was thinking about Bonita, the one I knew and considered my friend…until that night. I was so full of hurt and anger that I refused to consider something else might be wrong. I was mistaken about you and wrong about her, as well."

He turned her around to face him with hands firmly on her shoulders. "There was no way you or any of us could have known about her mental condition."

"But I was her friend, I should have known," she said.

"You aren't a mind reader. Grant lived with her, and he didn't have a clue. What happened to her was sad, but we have to move on and—"

"Forget the past," she snapped, pulling out of his arms.

"That might be easy for you to do, but everyone isn't as forgiving as you, Canyon."

He frowned, dropping his hands from her shoulders. "What are you talking about?"

"I hurt you. I kept Beau away from you, yet you've forgiven me. That's all well and good, but I can't forgive myself, Canyon. I can't. Every time I see you and Beau together I'm reminded of what I did, of how much pain I caused both of us. And now I see how I wronged Bonita—"

"Whoa. I won't let you take the blame for that. Bonita had a mental illness that you didn't know about. Will you stop allowing misplaced blame to rule your life? To rule our life?"

She wiped a tear from her eye. "There's no *our life,* Canyon."

He stared at her. "What do you mean?"

"I mean that until I can come to terms with what I did and let it go there can't be an *us.*"

He shook his head, as if dismissing what she'd said. "Of course there can be an *us.* We had a son together. You love me, and I love you."

She lifted her chin. "Do you really? How can you when I find it hard to love myself."

Canyon drew in a deep breath in an effort to make some sense of what she was saying. "Correct me if I'm wrong, but did we not make love in that bed last night? Did we not make love at your place today? And in that bed over there again tonight?"

She turned away with slumped shoulders, but not before she said, "Doesn't matter."

He turned her back around to face him. "Yes, it does matter," he said fiercely. "And when things matter, you don't give up. You make it work. I refuse to let you become a victim of negativity and guilt. I refuse to let you punish yourself for something that wasn't your fault."

Canyon looked out the window at the sky to find the strength he needed where she was concerned. He loved her with all his heart, and he refused to let her give up on them.

He looked back down at her. "Do you love me, Keisha?"

She swiped back tears. "Yes, I love you" she said softly. "But this is one of those times when loving someone might not be enough."

"I love you, and I have it from the best—my married brothers and cousins—that loving someone will always be enough," he said. "More than enough," he added, cupping her face in his hands.

"But, baby, you have to believe it. You have to get off this guilt trip you're on, and stop believing you're to blame for every damn thing that goes wrong. You're not perfect and neither am I. We've both made mistakes. Everyone has."

His eyes held hers. "What I want more than anything is to marry you. Not because of Beau, but because of us. We're back together for a reason, Keisha, and I want to believe it's because that's where we should be. I want more than just Beau. I want us to have other kids, more Westmorelands to one day rule this land. Tell me you'll marry me."

He watched how her lips trembled and the look in her eyes reflected uncertainty.

When she didn't answer, he dropped his hands and took a step back. "I need to get away for a while. I'm going over to Stern's Stronghold. I'll be back later."

"But it's almost midnight," she said.

He shrugged as he slid into his jeans and put on his shirt. "He's a late-nighter." After slipping into his shoes, he said, "Go to bed and get some sleep."

Canyon left the room, taking the stairs two at a time.

Before walking out the door he grabbed his cell phone off the table and saw he'd missed several calls. Only then did he remember that he'd placed it on vibrate while they'd been at McKays. Deciding he would check the missed calls later, he breathed in the mountain air the moment his foot touched his porch.

Lord knows he was trying to be patient with Keisha, but she was wearing him thin. He didn't want her for a lover. He wanted her as his wife. Canyon figured that until she came to terms with the issue of her father she would be weighed down by her inability to forgive, even when the only one needing that forgiveness was herself.

As he unlocked the door and got into his car he knew he would do whatever it took to make her see that while he'd gone without her for three years, now that she and Beau were in his life, he didn't intend to do without either one of them again.

Canyon's mind was so full of thoughts of Keisha and the marriage proposal she hadn't accepted that he didn't notice the dark vehicle deliberately hidden behind the tall sagebrush as he left Canyon's Bluff.

Thirteen

Keisha slid into her robe, tightening the belt around her waist when she heard the sound of Canyon's car driving away. The last thing she would be able to do was take his suggestion and get some sleep, so she decided to go downstairs for a cup of tea. She grabbed her cell phone off the nightstand planning to chat with her Mom. Knowing how her mother kept late hours, Keisha figured she would still be up.

She saw she had missed a couple of calls from Detective Render and wondered if he'd tried calling her because there was a new development with her case. It was too late to return his call tonight, but she would do so first thing in the morning. She had promised Canyon that she would stay here a week and she had four days left. Her plans were to return home on Saturday. Thanks to Canyon her home was back in order, along with a new security system. She was glad because she refused to live in fear that someone out there wanted to do her harm.

Yet, you're willing to live in another kind of fear, her mind mocked. *Fear of your own vulnerability.*

Keisha took a sip of the tea she'd just brewed and sat down at the kitchen table. *And what about your inability to forgive? That's the root of your problem. Are you trying to hold yourself to a higher standard than most people? Forgiving yourself for mistakes isn't a crime. Maybe you ought to try it.*

Keisha sighed as she clicked her phone to call her mother. Lynn picked up within two rings.

"Keisha? You okay?"

She knew her mother found it odd that she was calling so late and Keisha quickly assured her she was fine. "Yes, I'm okay. I couldn't sleep."

"What's bothering you?"

Keisha then told her mother what Grant had told her and Canyon about Bonita.

Lynn said, "It wasn't your fault, what happened to Bonita, and Canyon has forgiven you for the other mistakes, so why are you tormenting yourself? Why is it easier to deny yourself the man you love than it is for you to forgive anyone who you feel has done you wrong?"

"Someone like Kenneth Drew?"

There was a moment of silence on the other end of the phone and Keisha figured it was time she and her mother had *that* talk. "So, tell me, Mom, when was the last time you saw him?" She'd never asked her mother anything about the man who was her father.

"I saw him today in fact."

Keisha nodded. That didn't surprise her. "So you've forgiven him?"

"Yes, I had to move on."

"Move on? Is that why you're seeing him again?"

She heard her mother's sharp intake of breath. Keisha drew in a deep breath of her own and then said softly, "You gave yourself away without meaning to and that's okay. You don't need my permission do anything, you know. I just don't want you to get hurt again."

"It might be hard for you to understand now, baby, but one day you will see that life is something you won't be able to hang on to forever. That cancer scare three years ago showed me that. You should embrace life every day, with no regrets. Kenneth and I both made mistakes and he knows he's hurt me. He knows he's hurt you. He has tried to make things right."

"How? Just by claiming me as his because I look like him? Where was he when I was in school and you had to struggle to support me? What about when I was in college and law school and—"

"He paid for that."

Keisha stopped talking. "Excuse me?"

"Kenneth never wanted me to tell you, but he's the one who paid your college tuition. All of it. Including law school. At first I wasn't going to accept his offer, but I knew it was something he wanted to do. He and I both knew it wouldn't erase the first fifteen years of your life, but he was hell-bent on giving you everything he could during the years after that."

Keisha was silent. All this time she'd assumed her mother had been too independent to accept anything from anyone, especially from a man who'd turned his back on her when she had needed him the most.

"And another thing, Keisha," her mother said. "He never married and neither did I. You're his only child, and he says I'm the only woman he ever truly loved. He wants a life with me and doesn't think it's too late."

Keisha swallowed. "And what do you want, Mom?" she asked softly.

There was a pause and then, "I want him, too. But then, I don't want to lose my daughter."

Keisha hung her head. She should not be placing her mother in a position where she felt she had to choose. Could Keisha handle being the cause of her mother's unhappiness?

"Mom, I want you to be happy. Do what makes you happy. And no matter what, I will always be your daughter. Nothing will ever change that." Keisha stood. "I made some tea and I need to finish it off and get back to bed. We'll talk again later this week."

"Okay. They still haven't found out who trashed your home?"

"No, but I feel certain that they will. It's just a matter of time. Denver has a wonderful police force."

After ending the call to her mother, Keisha headed for the front door with her cup of tea. She had enjoyed sitting on the porch last night. But then of course Canyon had been with her. Tonight he had been in a hurry to flee her presence. Opening the door, she drew in a deep breath. This was something she'd missed while living in Austin. The air was fresh, as well as calming and comforting, things she needed right now.

Leaning against a post, she sipped her tea, watched the sky and tried to put her conversation with her mother to the back of her mind for now. She marveled at Canyon's fascination with the solar system and knew there was a star up there he claimed as his. Well, now she would claim it as hers, as well. He believed the star had helped get him through a number of rough times in his life. Maybe that same star could help her.

There was a moon tonight and stars aplenty. She wondered which one was Canyon's. She figured it had to be the one that was the biggest and the brightest since he was known to do things on a grand scale.

She'd never wished upon a star but hopefully it wasn't too late to do so. Closing her eyes she made a wish, one that was her heart's most ardent desire. She loved Canyon, and he loved her. They had a son to raise together, and tonight he'd asked her to marry him.

Opening her eyes she looked up at the star and said aloud, "One of you up there is Canyon's star and I'm making you mine, as well. I will be more forgiving, and I won't blame myself for everything. I forgive myself. I am not to blame."

She smiled, feeling renewed. Rejuvenated. Taking another sip of tea, she turned around and then gasped, dropping the cup. She tried to steady her breath and calm her heart rate. She recognized the man standing there.

Keisha opened her mouth to ask him what he was doing there, but stopped when he said in an accusing tone, "You're wrong. You *are* to blame. You're to blame for everything that has gone wrong in my life."

"Is there a reason why you're visiting me at this hour?"

Canyon ignored Stern's question as he studied the picture frames lined across the fireplace mantel. He asked a question of his own. "Do the women, the ones you bring here to the Stronghold, ever ask why you have so many photographs of you and JoJo around this place?"

Stern chuckled. "Trying to change the subject, are we? Okay, I'll give you this one. First of all, it's none of their business. And second, they don't question me because they know better. My friendship with JoJo is never to be questioned."

Now it was Canyon's turn to chuckle as he turned

around to face his brother. "Why? Because then you'll have to explain how she kept Steven Edison from beating you up that day when the two of you were in middle school. Or how the only reason you won that high school swim trophy you still like to brag about is because she was on your team? Or how she is responsible for keeping your Corvette running like a charm? Or how—"

"Now, why are you here again?" Stern interrupted to ask.

Canyon plopped down into the chair. "I like visiting you after midnight."

"That's bull and you know it. You have a tendency to hang out at the Bluff as if you're guarding the place." Stern smiled. "But that was before it was invaded by Keisha and my man Beau. I like him by the way. I plan on teaching him how to race cars when he grows up."

Canyon rolled his eyes. That was when he remembered those missed calls. It was too late to return them, but at least he could check to see who'd tried contacting him earlier that evening. Shifting his body, he pulled the phone out of his back pocket and noticed all three calls had been from Detective Render. There was also a text message... Call me when you see this text. No matter how late.

"Detective Render wants me to call him," he said to Stern.

"Now?"

Canyon shrugged. "The text said no matter how late. Must be important." He clicked on the detective's number and after two rings Render answered.

"Render, this is Canyon."

"I tried calling earlier," Render said.

"I went out to dinner and had my phone on vibrate and didn't hear it. What's up?"

"First, none of Ms. Ashford's coworkers in Austin are

being harassed so we don't feel it's connected to her former job. But there is something else we're checking out.
Ms. Ashford's neighborhood has one of those monitoring
video cameras at the entrance, and we noticed this car on
her street the same day her house was trashed...and we
also noticed it returned the day after and the day after that,
as if checking the status of her home."

Canyon nodded. "Possibly a visitor to someone in Keisha's neighborhood."

"That's what we assumed but we pulled license plate
records and this person made us curious."

"Why?"

"Because he works at the law firm with Ms. Ashford.
We did some further checking, and although he's a model
employee, his personal life turned to shambles a few years
ago when his wife discovered he was involved in an illicit
affair and filed for divorce. She actually caught him on
a video having sex in their bedroom one weekend when
she was out of town. She filed a restraining order last
year when he kept harassing her, trying to get her to take
him back."

Canyon rubbed his jaw, feeling tired and wondering
where Render was going with this—until this particular
story started to sound familiar. Mainly the part about a
man being caught by his wife on video, having an affair.
"Wait a minute," Canyon said, straightening in his chair.
"What's the man's name?"

"Michael Jarrod. We went to his place to question him,
and he wasn't home. Talked to his neighbor, who said she
hadn't seen him all day. And we found out that he left early
from work, claiming he'd gotten sick. You know him?"

"No, but today someone mentioned a man who had an
affair with his fiancée and the details were oddly similar. I need to check on something, and I'll call you back."

Canyon clicked off and went through the contact list on his phone. Lucky for him he had exchanged phone numbers with Grant before the man had left their table to rejoin his friends. Canyon clicked on the number. It was late but…

"Hello."

The man answered in a very sleepy voice. "Grant, this is Canyon. Sorry to bother you at this hour but something important came up, and I wondered if you can tell me the name of the married man that Bonita had an affair with."

"Yes," Grant said groggily. "His name was Michael! Jarrod."

A funny feeling settled in Canyon's stomach. "Thanks, and again I'm sorry I woke you."

Canyon then called Render back and told him of the conversation with Grant at dinner. "I don't know why a man who works with Keisha who had an affair with a woman who was once Keisha's best friend would be coming into her neighborhood, three times in one week, but I'm going to find out. Maybe Keisha can shed some light on it," Canyon said, standing. He ended his call with Render.

Stern stared up at Canyon when he saw the concerned look on his brother's face. "Something's wrong?"

Canyon was headed for the door. "No. I just need to talk to Keisha about something. I'll talk to you later."

"Michael? What are you talking about and what are you doing here?"

Michael Jarrod came to stand in the moonlight and the look on his face was so serious that for the first time since knowing him, Keisha felt uncomfortable. "I'm talking about your friend. Bonita," he said.

Keisha lifted a brow. "Bonita? What about Bonita?" She vaguely recalled introducing Bonita and Michael several years ago, when Bonita had dropped by the firm. As far as she knew, their paths never crossed again.

"That day you introduced us, she seemed nice and well mannered. Someone with class. So imagine my shock when I was at a club one night with friends and she walked in, ready to sleep with the first man she saw. We ended up having an affair that lasted three months before my wife found out. Linda divorced me and refuses to take me back, and it's all your fault for introducing me to that woman."

Keisha thought she'd heard everything. But never had she heard anything so ridiculous in her life. Even *she* wouldn't claim blame for that one. "Michael, think about what you just said. *You* are responsible for your own actions. Introducing Bonita to you didn't push you into betraying your wife by sleeping with her. That was *your* doing and not mine."

She tried keeping the anger out of her voice. Her going on a guilt trip of her own doing was one thing, but she refused to let someone else send her on one unjustly.

"Besides," she added. "Bonita had a split personality. That's the reason she displayed one personality when you met her that day and another when you ran into her that night at the club."

"And you want me to believe that?"

"It's true."

He frowned. "Then you should have told me."

"I just found out recently." She'd never known Michael to display anger. He'd been a really nice guy when she'd lived in Denver before. But she had noticed since she'd returned that he'd been less friendly and more withdrawn. One of the other attorneys at the firm had mentioned that Michael had gotten a divorce but hadn't provided any details. Keisha figured the divorce was the reason he had started keeping to himself.

"But that's not the only thing I'm blaming you for." Michael broke into her thoughts.

Keisha was feeling more uncomfortable. Michael had no reason to be here, at one in the morning, standing outside on Canyon's porch. Why was he here and how did he know where to find her? She hadn't told any of her coworkers or Mr. Spivey where she was staying. Had he followed her? And why had he showed up when Canyon wasn't here? Was that deliberate?

"You left the firm right before I started going through my divorce," Michael said, interrupting her thoughts. "To deal with the mess my life was in, I threw myself into my work and took on cases nobody else wanted. I felt I had a good shot at making partner. Then you messed things up by coming back. You were Spivey and Whitlock's golden girl before. They thought you walked on water, and they were overjoyed when you decided to come back. They brag about the job you're doing just because you've won a few cases. Now rumor around the firm says that you'll make partner before I do. I was there when you got there. I was there when you left. It's not fair, and it's all your fault."

Keisha knew there was no sense wasting her time telling Michael just how ridiculous he sounded. The man had issues, which only made her more concerned about him and why he was here. "There's nothing I can say that will make you see how unjust your claims are. I suggest you leave now."

His smile sent chills up her body. "Oh, I'm leaving, and I'm taking you with me. I tried sending you warnings by paying that guy to scare you on the road and I, along with a friend who knew how to bypass your alarm system, even wrecked your house, hoping you would get scared and hightail it back to Texas. But this morning Spivey an-

nounced you were out and would return in a week. That's
not good enough."

Fury fired through Keisha's veins. "You're the one who
did those things? How dare you! I never did anything to
you, and you trashed my house, turned my and my son's
world upside down because of misplaced blame? How dare
you?"

"Yes, how dare me?" he mocked. "You can get mad
but it doesn't matter. I saw your boyfriend leave and since
you didn't take my other warnings I'm getting rid of you
once and for all. I'm not going to kill you. I plan to turn
you over to some people I know involved in human traf-
ficking to Central America. They'll toy with you a while,
shoot you up with drugs and destroy that sharp mind of
yours, the one that Spivey and Whitlock admire so much.
No one will able be able to find you."

Keisha took a step back. Michael wasn't thinking
straight. "I'm not going anywhere with you."

"You don't have a choice. I don't want to hurt you," he
said. "But I will."

And then she saw it. The steel blade of the knife he was
holding glinted in the moonlight. Fear rose in her throat.
"Michael, please. You're not thinking straight. Nobody can
place all the blame on others for their own actions." *Like
nobody should place all the blame on themselves either.
Or not forgive others, or themselves, when they have the
chance to do so.*

"Let's go. No telling when your boyfriend will return,"
Michael said.

Keisha had hoped she could keep him talking until Canyon came back. All she could think about was Beau upstairs sleeping. She had to keep him safe. "Michael, please.
I am not to blame for all your problems. We were once
friends and—"

"No! A friend would not have ruined my marriage or taken away a job that should be mine! Now move!"

Knowing she had no choice, Keisha began walking down the steps from the porch. She knew she had to think of something fast when she saw his car. Once he got her inside it she might never get away.

An idea came into her head when she saw the weed edger that Canyon had used the other day, resting against a tree. It was a chance she had to take. Pretending to almost stumble, she quickly grabbed hold of the edger and twirled around fast, swinging it wide, feeling victorious when the knife was knocked out of his hand.

Instead of retrieving it, Michael lunged for her. She swung again, going low with all her might, hitting his knee hard and sending him to the ground. He scrambled to get up and she swung again. He was almost successful in grabbing the edger from her hand, but she kicked him below the belt. He yelped, releasing the edger. But he was looking around for the knife. She thought of running for the house but wasn't sure she could make it. So she continued to use the tool she had, swinging it back and forth. When he tried charging for her, she hit the power switch and set the blades in motion.

"Put that down, bitch!" he screamed, backing up when she almost shoved the blades in his face.

"I won't! And I'm not to blame. Do you hear me? I am not to blame!" She screamed at the top of her lungs, moving closer to his face with the blades.

She didn't notice when Canyon arrived, but he was there, coming up behind Michael and knocking him to the ground with one hard blow. Michael tried to get away from Canyon but that meant staring into the edger's blades.

So he turned and tried fighting Canyon, who with another single hard blow, knocked Michael out cold. It was only then that Keisha cut the switch to the edger and ran straight into Canyon's arms.

"You okay, baby?" he asked, holding her close.

"Yes, I'm okay. His name is Michael Jarrod and I work with him. He's the one who trashed my house and paid that guy to scare me on the road."

"I know, baby. I know."

She leaned back. "You know?"

"Yes. I had several missed calls from Render on my phone and called him. I figured things out and came back to ask you about Jarrod. I had no idea he was here. I should not have gotten mad and left tonight, leaving you and Beau alone. I don't want to think what could have happened."

She cupped his face. "Don't blame yourself. Michael was crazy, blaming me for things that were his fault. He blamed me for introducing him to Bonita, which resulted in an affair and his divorce, and he blamed me because Mr. Spivey is considering me for partner, a position he felt he deserved."

Canyon nodded, pulled out his phone and punched in Render's number. When Render answered, he said, "I think you need to come to my place and bring the police with you. Michael Jerrod tried to kidnap Keisha."

Canyon then called Stern. "Bring your rope. I need your help in tying up the man who tried to kidnap Keisha."

Putting his phone back in his pocket, he saw Jerrod was still out cold. He then turned his attention back to Keisha. "You meant everything you were screaming at Jarrod?"

She lifted an arched brow. "What?"

"Basically, that you won't blame yourself for anything again?"

She drew in a deep breath and nodded. "Yes, I meant it. I was saved by your star."

He looked at her oddly. "What?"

"I'll tell you later. Right now I just need you to hold me some more."

Canyon gathered her close and wrapped her in his arms.

Fourteen

Keisha learned that night that nobody in their right mind messed with a Westmoreland. Michael learned that lesson as well when he'd regained consciousness. Stern and Canyon had approached to tie him up, and he thought he could use that same edger on them that she had used on him. Not only had they taken the edger from him, but they had whipped his behind doing so.

Other Westmorelands had arrived as well as the police and Detective Render. She had felt sad watching a hand-cuffed Michael placed in the back of a police cruiser. He was a brilliant attorney who'd lost his bearings and she hoped he got the help he needed. Yes, she even felt she had the ability to forgive him for what he did. Like Bonita, he was mentally unstable.

"You okay?"

She glanced over at Canyon. After everyone had left,

they had taken a shower together and gotten into bed. Beau, bless his heart, had slept through it all.

"I'm fine," she said, cuddling closer to him. They had made love in the shower but she knew they would be making love again before either of them drifted off to sleep.

"Canyon?"

"Yes, sweetheart?"

"I love you so much, and I know I won't be able to change completely overnight. But I know I can accept things I wasn't able to accept before. My faults as well as others'. Making a wish upon your star helped."

"You mentioned my star earlier, and I wondered what you meant."

She told him what she'd been doing outside on the porch before turning around to find Michael. "I know I'm not perfect and will make mistakes, but I won't accept the blame for everything." She paused a moment and then added. "And I will do better in the forgiving department. I've sort of forgiven Michael already."

"What about your father?"

She didn't say anything for a minute, thinking of the phone call she'd had with her mother earlier. "I want to move forward with him, as well. It won't be easy but I'm willing to try. Mom has, and if she can forgive him then so can I. She's the one he hurt more than anyone else."

Canyon then turned her to face him. "I hate to say I'm saving the best for last, but now, what about me? Earlier tonight I asked you to marry me and you didn't give me an answer. Are you ready to give me an answer now?"

She smiled. "Yes. I'm more than ready."

He took her hand in his. "Keisha Ashford, would you marry me? Be my wife? Live here with me, share my life, give me more babies and love me as much as I love you?"

She fought back her tears. "Yes, I will marry you, Canyon. I want all those things that you want and more. I love you and I need you more than I ever thought was possible."

A huge smile spread across Canyon's lips. "Riley and Alpha are getting married next month, and Zane and Channing will tie the knot at Christmas. I want us to marry now. My son will have my name and I want his mother to have my name, as well. If you want a big wedding then we—"

"No, I don't need or want a big wedding. I prefer something small with your family and mine. Here at Canyon's Bluff." Her eyes lit up. "At night. Under the stars. Our star."

Canyon leaned down and covered Keisha's mouth with his and she knew from this day forward. She was his, completely.

Epilogue

Two weeks later

"When one mentions a wedding night, Canyon, this is not exactly what comes to mind," Stern said, glancing over at his brother.

Canyon chuckled as he glanced up at the sky. It was a beautiful August night and the moon was full, adding light to the lit torches that lined his driveway and decorated his huge porch.

Someone, and he'd figured it had been his female cousins, sisters- and cousins-in-law, had decorated the porch with huge white ribbons and sky-blue latex balloons. The balloons represented the color the sky would have been had they gotten married during the day. But they had chosen to get married at night.

"I see Flash," he said and then gave Stern his attention. "Tell Pam to let Keisha know Flash is here so we can begin."

Stern arched a brow. "Who's Flash?"

"Our star."

Fifteen minutes later Alpha Blake had everything ready. Canyon thought it was pretty damn nice to have an event planner in the family. Although she was in the middle of planning her own wedding, Alpha had gone right to work when Keisha had told Alpha of her desire to have a night-time wedding. He was amazed at what had been done in just two weeks.

They had only invited family and close friends and a reception would follow. Tomorrow he and Keisha would leave to spend a few days in Vegas and return to Denver to get Beau for a trip to Disneyland.

He had asked Dillon to be his best man, and Keisha's mother was her matron of honor. Her father would be walking her out of the house and down the porch steps to where Canyon was standing. Canyon liked Kenneth Drew and knew the man was sincere in wanting to reconcile with his daughter. Kenneth was already overwhelmed with Beau.

Canyon was speechless when Keisha had told him that the world-famous attorney Kenneth Drew was her father. Drew's reputation rivaled that of Johnnie Cochran. He was best known for winning a number of notable cases.

Canyon held his breath when his front door opened and Lynn walked out to the instrumental rendition of "Music of the Night" from *Phantom of the Opera* flowing softly through the air. Ramsey's daughter, Susan, followed, carrying a small basket of flowers and tossing them to and fro. Then came Beau and Denver who grabbed more than a few chuckles when once their little feet hit the last step, they raced across the yard to their fathers, clearly disobeying the orders Alpha had whispered to them earlier to walk and not run. Everyone had been concerned the wedding would take place way past the kids' bedtimes and the parents had made sure the kids had taken an extra-long nap today.

Keisha appeared in the doorway on her father's arm. She had decided to wear a beautiful light blue tea-length dress. At that moment, Canyon thought she was the most beautiful woman he'd ever seen. Her father walked her to the last step and then she crossed the yard to Canyon alone. When she reached him, he took her hand, stared at her for a moment, lifted her hand to his lips and kissed it. Then together they both stared up into the sky, saw Flash and then smiled at each other before turning to the minister to be joined as man and wife beneath the beautiful Denver stars.

Canyon nibbled kisses along the side of his wife's neck. Keisha turned her head and whispered, "Canyon, behave. There are people looking at us."

He chuckled. "Let them look. Maybe they will take the hint it's time for them to leave. I'm beginning to think having the reception here in our home wasn't a good idea."

Flutters raced through Keisha. *Their home.* She was now the mistress of this, Canyon's Bluff. She had taken a two-month leave from work and Mr. Spivey and Mr. Whitlock understood. Everyone had been as shocked as she'd been over Michael's behavior, and everyone was glad he was getting the mental-health treatment he needed.

"I hate to interrupt this unprecedented show of passion, but Pam would like to talk to Keisha in the house for a minute," Stern said.

Canyon gave Keisha a kiss before she left and then he turned to Stern. "So, you're on vacation next week. Got anything planned?"

Stern shrugged. "I'm headed for the lodge to do some elk hunting in Woodland Park."

Canyon lifted a brow. "Alone?"

"No. JoJo is going with me."

Canyon nodded. A few years ago Stern had purchased a run-down hunting lodge that he had since restored. It was now a beauty and Stern rented it out except for those times he used it himself. "Well, don't let JoJo outhunt you, like she did the last time."

Stern smiled. "I'll try not to, but you know JoJo, anything a man can do she can probably do better."

At that moment, Keisha returned. She had changed into a green pantsuit. She slid car keys into Canyon's hand. "I'm ready to go."

Canyon lifted a brow. "We're going somewhere? Tonight?"

Keisha chuckled. "Yes. That was my surprise for you. I made reservations for us at a hotel in town. Our bags are packed already and in the car. Mom and Dad will take care of things until we return tomorrow."

Grinning, Canyon took Keisha's hand. The idea of sneaking off from his own wedding reception was an awesome surprise. "Then, what are we waiting for? Let's go, baby."

He turned to Stern. "Enjoy your vacation, and I'll see you when you get back."

Canyon then tightened his hand on Keisha's as they walked to his car. He was more than ready to get her alone. She was his heart and his soul. His everything. And when he got her into that hotel room, he intended to prove it.

* * * * *

*Don't miss the next Westmoreland novel
by Brenda Jackson!
STERN
When Stern Westmoreland helps his best friend with a
makeover, he never expects sizzling attraction to ignite
between them. Now there's only one way to make her
his—have one long, steamy night together as much
more than friends!*

COMING NEXT MONTH from Harlequin Desire®
AVAILABLE SEPTEMBER 3, 2013

#2251 STERN
The Westmorelands
Brenda Jackson
After his best friend's makeover, Stern Westmoreland suddenly wants her all for himself! Will he prove they can be much more than friends?

#2252 SOMETHING ABOUT THE BOSS...
Texas Cattleman's Club: The Missing Mogul
Yvonne Lindsay
Sophie suspects her new boss is involved in his business partner's disappearance, and she'll risk it all to uncover the truth...even if she has to seduce it out of him.

#2253 THE NANNY TRAP
Billionaires and Babies
Cat Schield
When his wife deserts their child, Blake hires the baby's surrogate mother as nanny—and desire unexpectedly ignites between them. But when the nanny reveals her secret, everything changes!

#2254 BRINGING HOME THE BACHELOR
The Bolton Brothers
Sarah M. Anderson
When the reformed "Wild" Bill Bolton finds himself as the prize at a charity bachelor auction, he has good girl Jenny thinking about taking a walk on the wild side!

#2255 CONVENIENTLY HIS PRINCESS
Married by Royal Decree
Olivia Gates
Aram's convenient bride turns out to be most inconvenient when he falls in love with her! But will Kanza believe in their love when the truth comes out?

#2256 A BUSINESS ENGAGEMENT
Duchess Diaries
Merline Lovelace
Sarah agreed to a fake engagement to save her sister, but the sexy business tycoon she's promised to—and the magic of Paris—make it all too real!

You can find more information on upcoming Harlequin® titles, free excerpts and more at www.Harlequin.com.

HDCNM0813

REQUEST YOUR FREE BOOKS!
2 FREE NOVELS PLUS 2 FREE GIFTS!

HARLEQUIN®

Desire

ALWAYS POWERFUL, PASSIONATE AND PROVOCATIVE

YES! Please send me 2 FREE Harlequin Desire® novels and my 2 FREE gifts (gifts are worth about $10). After receiving them, if I don't wish to receive any more books, I can return the shipping statement marked "cancel." If I don't cancel, I will receive 6 brand-new novels every month and be billed just $4.55 per book in the U.S. or $4.99 per book in Canada. That's a savings of at least 13% off the cover price! It's quite a bargain! Shipping and handling is just 50¢ per book in the U.S. and 75¢ per book in Canada.* I understand that accepting the 2 free books and gifts places me under no obligation to buy anything. I can always return a shipment and cancel at any time. Even if I never buy another book, the two free books and gifts are mine to keep forever.

225/326 HDN F4ZC

Name _____ (PLEASE PRINT) _____

Address _____ Apt. # _____

City _____ State/Prov. _____ Zip/Postal Code _____

Signature (if under 18, a parent or guardian must sign)

Mail to the **Harlequin® Reader Service:**
IN U.S.A.: P.O. Box 1867, Buffalo, NY 14240-1867
IN CANADA: P.O. Box 609, Fort Erie, Ontario L2A 5X3

Want to try two free books from another line?
Call 1-800-873-8635 or visit www.ReaderService.com.

* Terms and prices subject to change without notice. Prices do not include applicable taxes. Sales tax applicable in N.Y. Canadian residents will be charged applicable taxes. Offer not valid in Quebec. This offer is limited to one order per household. Not valid for current subscribers to Harlequin Desire books. All orders subject to credit approval. Credit or debit balances in a customer's account(s) may be offset by any other outstanding balance owed by or to the customer. Please allow 4 to 6 weeks for delivery. Offer available while quantities last.

Your Privacy—The Harlequin® Reader Service is committed to protecting your privacy. Our Privacy Policy is available online at www.ReaderService.com or upon request from the Harlequin Reader Service.

We make a portion of our mailing list available to reputable third parties that offer products we believe may interest you. If you prefer that we not exchange your name with third parties, or if you wish to clarify or modify your communication preferences, please visit us at www.ReaderService.com/consumerchoice or write to us at Harlequin Reader Service Preference Service, P.O. Box 9062, Buffalo, NY 14269. Include your complete name and address.

HDI3R

SPECIAL EXCERPT FROM

 HARLEQUIN®

Desire

A sneak peek at

STERN, *a Westmoreland novel*

by **New York Times** *and* **USA TODAY** *bestselling author*

Brenda Jackson

Available September 2013.
Only from Harlequin® Desire!

As far as Stern was concerned, his best friend had lost her ever-loving mind. But he didn't say that. Instead, he asked, "What's his name?"

"You don't need to know that. Do you tell me the name of every woman you want?"

"This is different."

"Really? In what way?"

He wasn't sure, but he just knew that it was. "For you to even ask me, that means you're not ready for the kind of relationship you're going after."

JoJo threw her head back and laughed. "Stern, I'll be thirty next year. I'm beginning to think that most of the men in town wonder if I'm really a girl."

He studied her. There had never been any doubt in his mind that she was a girl. She had long lashes and eyes so dark they were the color of midnight. She had gorgeous legs, long and endless. But he knew he was one of the few men who'd ever seen them.

"You hide what a nice body you have," he finally said. He suddenly sat up straight in the rocker. "I have an idea.

What you need is a makeover."

"A makeover?"

"Yes, and then you need to go where your guy hangs out. In a dress that shows your legs, in a style that shows off your hair." He reached over and took the cap off her head. Lustrous dark brown hair tumbled to her shoulders. He smiled. "See, I like it already."

And he did. He was tempted to run his hands through it to feel the silky texture.

He leaned back and took another sip of his beer, wondering where such a tempting thought had come from. This was JoJo, for heaven's sake. His best friend. He should not be thinking about how silky her hair was.

He should not be bothered by the thought of men checking out JoJo, of men calling her for a date.

Suddenly, he was thinking that maybe a makeover wasn't such a great idea after all.

Will Stern help JoJo win her dream man?

STERN

by New York Times *and* USA TODAY
bestselling author Brenda Jackson

*Available September 2013
Only from Harlequin® Desire!*

Desire

ALWAYS POWERFUL, PASSIONATE AND PROVOCATIVE.

THE NANNY TRAP

Cat Schield

A Billionaires & Babies novel: Powerful men...
wrapped around their babies' little fingers

When his wife deserts their child, Blake hires the baby's
surrogate mother as nanny—and desire unexpectedly
ignites between them. But when the nanny reveals her
secret, everything changes!

Look for *THE NANNY TRAP* next month by
Cat Schield, only from Harlequin® Desire.

Available wherever books and ebooks are sold.

HD73266

HARLEQUIN®

Desire

ALWAYS POWERFUL, PASSIONATE AND PROVOCATIVE.

CONVENIENTLY HIS PRINCESS

Olivia Gates

**Part of the Married by Royal Decree series:
When the king commands, they say "I do!"**

Aram's convenient bride turns out to be most
inconvenient when he falls in love with her! But will
Kanza believe in their love when the truth comes out?

Find out next month in
CONVENIENTLY HIS PRINCESS by Olivia Gates,
only from Harlequin® Desire.

Available wherever books and ebooks are sold.

HD73268

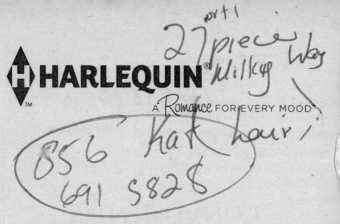